PHANTOM

PHANTOM

A NOVEL

BY

GERHART HAUPTMANN

TRANSLATED BY

BAYARD QUINCY MORGAN

NEW YORK   B. W. HUEBSCH, Inc.   MCMXXII

PHANTOM

I

My wife has furnished for me the tiny corner-room in the front, and I am now sitting in it. Across the way the village brook murmurs under ash and willow. Below me I hear the tinkling bell of the little shop which my wife tends It does well and supplies our modest demands completely.

But I shall have to undertake something besides. First, I have time to spare, and then I have spiritual cravings. Otherwise I am quite content and feel as happy as a king.

I smoke a pipe. That costs me virtually nothing, for we have cheap tobacco in the shop. Smoking stimulates the fancy. It also quiets. I get by it, for example, the opportunity to feel a state of agreeable leisure and at the same time to set down my thoughts in writing. "Why

[1]

don't you write," says my wife, "perhaps it may turn out to be a book, you know."

I just simply write down everything that passes through my mind.

And if I should succeed in making a book, why shouldn't I be able to write a second, a third? Then I should be an author. In the most natural way I should then have found my desired avocation.

This house, which my father-in-law bought six months ago, together with the shop, did once belong to the widow of such a person. Her name was Mrs. Wander. Wander was a schoolmaster who had had to give up his position on account of certain views. After long wanderings he found this asylum, like me, and had a livelihood in it. His life-work, which he may have begun and completed in this very room, is a German dictionary of proverbs in five volumes.

II

I AM unknown here so far. My wife and her father picked out this little village in the Hirschberg Valley, because they did not wish people to have constant occasion to talk about my "aimless journeys," [1] but also for the sake of withdrawing me from an environment which at every step must waken recollections in me, and keep them awake.

Just here it occurs to me: am I not on the point of thwarting their intention?

Yes and no.

If I reflect here upon my destiny, seek to gain a comprehensive view of my past, and endeavor to set down veraciously all that seems memorable to me, it is for one thing an attempt to free myself from the spell of my recollections, and something very different from unwillingly falling under their spell once more, which would probably happen in Breslau.

I never wish to see that place again.

Perhaps a man would no longer be able to live after such experiences as mine, if all past

[1] Translator's note. Title of a popular novel by Gerstäcker.

[3]

events were not actually unreal. In no case does the past any longer affect us with the power of reality. I must proceed with great calmness, patience, and care, if I would still recall to my mind the details of my great experience. The last are of course the most vivid, whereas all those that precede my entrance into prison are much less clear, although much more important.

I SPENT six years, four months, and twenty-one days in prison. That is a hard fact, which I had rather put down at the outset. It would be more than disagreeable to me to have fraudulently won myself readers by concealing it, if a complete book should some day actually be born of the faded dream of my life. It will then remain a fact, and be it here expressly stated, that the writer has been a convict.

IV

I should quite certainly not be writing these
lines, indeed quite certainly no longer be living,
but for my present wife Marie, née Stark.
Stark is a common name. But it is natural to
say, as is the fact, that my present wife is not
only called Stark [i. e. *strong*], but is so, although in pure externals she is characterized by
a gentle and amiable nature. Her father was a
bookbinder. If his daughter has been strong,
she has also had in him and at all times a strong
support.

My father-in-law is eighty. He clerks in the
shop below. He is an admirable man.

We have here in the village a strange schoolmaster: a baptized Jew, Dr. Levine. His father
was a banker in Berlin and very wealthy. They
say that Dr. Levine renounced the greatest part
of his fortune in favor of his brothers and sisters.
He was state's attorney, and was to be promoted
to Attorney-General, when he suddenly resigned
and after suitable preparation was appointed
here as teacher in the grammar-school. Only
thus could he appease his social conscience, as

[6]

he puts it. As a favor my father-in-law still occasionally binds a book for Dr. Levine.

I have sometimes told Dr. Levine this and that about my past. He encourages me to write it down.

He has furnished a comfortable study in the gable of the schoolhouse. When I recently returned to him some bound volumes, he detained me. I had to smoke a cigar and drink a cup of coffee with him. It was then I showed him the picture.

My wife knows nothing of the picture.

I received this picture from Melitta.

You see, when my relations with Melitta were at their zenith, I had told her in a confidential hour of my weakness for Veronica Harlan, the daughter of the hardware-merchant. Melitta was good-natured. One day she was having her picture taken and saw this picture in the photographer's studio. It was not hard to persuade him to let her have it, as she found the child-face in the picture so uncommonly beautiful. Dr. Levine also found it uncommonly beautiful.

It is beautiful, truly, but thank God it has no more power over me.

[7]

"No more power over me."

This assertion must be modified.

To-day with God's aid I enjoy perfect health. This health I attained in three years of utter solitude in my prison cell, and subsequently, when I was employed in the prison library through the kindness of the chief warden. There I could also complete my education.

Since I am now enjoying perfect health, the little picture has no more power over me. When the original of this picture entered into her power over me I was twenty-eight years old, and, because sickly from childhood, still older in spirit. From childhood I have been sickly, I said; I became really sick about in my twenty-second year. I coughed much and for several years the cough always left blood on my handkerchief. This had however passed when my spiritual sickness began.

They say that the so-called "consumption," that is the lung-disease, intensifies the craving for love. But I can perhaps return to that later. Anyway, it is the affair of medical science to determine what influence the body has upon the soul.

So much I think I can say, that when the spark fell upon my soul, a vast pile of fuel had collected in both soul and body.

Now what sort of spark was it, and of what origin was that spark? Here I could choose between having it consist of divine or devilish fire, tracing its origin from heaven or hell. Strictly speaking, if I were still in a position to operate with these concepts, I should have no choice at all. For since this spark gave rise to a truly hellish conflagration, a Christian could never admit that it was a heavenly spark. And so indeed the prison chaplain, the Reverend Mr. Walkmiller, called it a hellish spark, and thereupon of course found it very easy to trace all the terrible consequences for me and others back to this incendiarism of Satan.

Such a simplification would not be in the interest of truth, which is my purpose.

Just now I have once more scanned attentively the picture of the thirteen-year-old daughter of the hardware-dealer, and I must say that it is of captivating charm. "Virgin, mother, queen!"

[9]

the Master [1] would say. A sacred image in itself. It would not be strange if pilgrimages
were made to it from far and near.

An orthodox Catholic might object that the
guile of the devil may have occasionally made
use even of the unsuspecting Virgin Mother, in
order to lure souls to destruction.

So when I said: the picture has no more power
over me, I meant that in the sense of its misuse
by the devil it has no more power over me.

[1] Translator's note: i. e. Goethe, see Faust II, 12102.

So much for Satan; to trouble him again will I hope be unnecessary.

I was simply burned to ashes, as it were, by a conflagration, because I was absolutely defenseless, after my mole-like existence, before the inrush of the divine flame.

But in so far as this picture is the reflection of the divine flame, it still has power over me, and will retain it until my death.

I first saw Veronica Harlan one noon, when I, a poor municipal clerk, was walking home as usual. Before the city hall of Breslau stands the whipping-post. There are rings on it, with which the child was playing. It was the twenty-eighth of May, a date which for many reasons, as you will understand, I cannot forget. Even when the passers-by began to notice her, the governess could not divert the interest of the child from the whipping-post. She tried repeatedly to lure away from the steps the strikingly beautiful creature with the flying, saffron-yellow hair. In vain. I only know that my hat flew from my head—some one had jostled me—and recall how the child burst into an irresistibly hearty laugh at it.

Without the experience of that moment, I should probably be to this day without reproach before the world, and sorrow upon sorrow would have been spared me. But there is a proverb, to be sure not a German one, in the collection of the excellent Wander: "Even my own sorrow is dearer to me than the happiness of another." And if I were asked whether I would rather not have had that morning's adventure, seemingly so harmless, yet so pregnant with consequences, I must needs reply:

I would rather yield up my life than that experience.

VII

THIS confession, to my former judges, would be equivalent to the expression of basest obduracy, to a man of average common sense, the expression of highest folly. If I live long enough and abide by my desire and present ability, until all has been said that can make a frank and full confession wholly frank and full, and if my judges shall one day read it, it may be that they will change their minds. They will perhaps recognize how distorted, how incomplete, how false my confession in the protocols really is. The man of average common sense, on the other hand, who has already declared me foolish, will in the end regard his opinion as confirmed. For my part, as I reflect on my task, reflect superficially to be sure, I cannot help seeing in it the problem of weaving together the story of a dunce, a fool, and a criminal.

Of course, in doing this, I myself hope to be able to rise above the dunce, the fool, and the criminal—or let us say, to cast off all three.

VIII

A WORD about my extraction.

My father was a tax-collector, and had under him the supervision of the brandy-distilleries. In his duties he was frequently treated to liquor, and had eventually become a pronounced toper.

As he was seldom at home, traveling about on business and dependent on hotels, the greatest part of his income was squandered, in addition to his travel allowance. Had he not had a stroke of apoplexy in the very nick of time, they would probably have driven him out of office, and mother would have lost her pension. She had already made up several deficits in the accounts, having to beg the necessary sums of Aunt Schwab, which was not easy.

My mother had a hard life.

Wholly disappointed by my father, almost wholly abandoned, and made wholly unhappy by him, she found solace in her children, as is common in such cases. She had two sons and a daughter. I was the oldest. As long as my brother and my sister, the youngest among us, were children, things went well enough. When they had passed their seventeenth or eighteenth year, it became absolutely clear that one could not rely on them any more. That was at the time when my mother was already in the fifth year of her widowhood.

I had always been on especially good terms with my mother. When this had begun, I do not know. I think very early. It was already so when I first observed that my father could not endure me. As he was also mostly at odds with my mother, I naturally took sides with her.

I cannot say when I became her avowed favorite. It must have been before father's death. Even then she often would call me her only comfort. Later, when I had become a solicitor's clerk and always put my whole pay into her hands on the first of the month, I would not infrequently hear her say that I was her only support.

The flat into which we moved after father's death was in the second story of an old-fashioned little house in Pocket Street. We kept it until the catastrophe came, that is for about eight years. It was very small, very dark, but nevertheless not uncomfortable. Such quaint little

[15]

city houses, with their small windows and low-ceiled rooms, usually have great charm. I had no idea but that I and my mother should live in those rooms till the end of our days.

I assumed in the little household the position of father, of head of the family. Considerably older than the other children, I was an authority to them for that reason alone. But more than this, my mother took every occasion to affirm my paternal power over them in their presence. It fell to me for another reason too, because I had long been the sole bread-winner. When my brother and my sister occasionally earned something themselves, they never turned over so much as a red cent to my mother.

This paternal authority I never misused, to my knowledge.

To spare my lungs and larynx I had accustomed myself to speak in a low voice. It became second nature with me. It is still clear in my mind how at the trial several of the jurors cried to me, "Louder, Louder!" This restrained manner of speech I never needed to accelerate or intensify in intercourse with my brother and sister, even when I had occasion to admonish or reprimand them. I may say that I enjoyed from them esteem mingled with admiration, and had a more unrestricted authority than even my father had ever possessed.

"You ought to teach, or rather, you ought to have become a teacher," my mother would say at times, when she noticed how I would take the trouble to hear my brother and sister recite dates in history, Bible verses, and the like. I am surely under no delusion in crediting myself with always having been to them a willing and patient adviser, helper, and teacher. And I took real pleasure in teaching.

Once when my mother had repeated her "You should have become a teacher," it occurred to me to wonder, I being then twenty-five, whether that were not still possible. The idea aroused my interest, nay my enthusiasm, in so far as one can call enthusiasm any one of the less depressed moods of which I was capable. Within a short time I had secured sufficient information, used for the first time a part of my wages to purchase books, and begun to spend every free hour in preparing myself to take the teacher's examination for secondary schools.

Until then I had lived along in a state of natural resignation, without thinking. While I was studying English, French, and the other subjects, both winter and summer in my cosy little room, the door of which opened on a wooden gallery above the little court, I was for the first time doing something which originated in a genuine initiative of my own. Hence I had a special gratification in it, and felt my self-confidence increasing.

I have not yet mentioned the double bone-fracture which I had had the misfortune to suffer as a child. My father had a military way of dealing with me which was hardly very appropriate in view of my gentle nature, with its tendency to subordination. When the name Lorenz, for so I was named, rang through the house in his accents, I almost always lost my head completely. Hurrying down a staircase in such a state of mind, I slipped and broke my leg. The bones were badly set by a quack, so that the affected leg became shorter. In order to repair the damage the leg was once more forcibly broken by another quack, whereupon it ultimately became still shorter. After that I limped, and that affected my way of life not a little, more especially at that time. For obvious reasons I avoided the children's games, in which I had so far taken part with enthusiasm, and turned to quiet occupations, preferably indoors and always where there was nobody present.

I think it was not until my trial that I really learned to think and to realize the blessing of independent thinking. Yet a beginning had been made when I formed the resolve to work towards the teaching profession, and as I have said, an indubitably increased self-confidence was the beneficial result of it.

IX

INDEED the self-instruction I had begun was beneficial to me in every respect, and I think back with pleasure on the hours I devoted to it. (My wife knows that, and has therefore tried to make this room as similar as possible to that in which I used to pursue my studies. The old tile-stove, against which I had shoved up my little study-table, was chocolate-brown. Perhaps at the advice of her father she has had this very similar stove set up for me, and by it stands the little old table once more.) Courses of instruction I procured by instalments. One by one I also purchased the other indispensable text-books. My mother vacillated the while between anxiety and approval. Her father was a prosperous citizen of Breslau, a furrier by trade, and the last four years before his death he had even been in the Council. Now to be sure she had resigned herself in every respect, but still it did flatter her self-esteem to see in me no longer the miserable clerk of a lawyer, but the future schoolmaster. On the other hand, the diminution of the household money, which she suffered in consequence of the book-buying, made itself painfully felt. Later, when my interest in literature and hence also for books developed beyond the range of teachers' courses, and I began to buy Reclam [1] editions and also somewhat more expensive editions of the classics, I sometimes found my mother in tears and had much difficulty in comforting and quieting her. To be sure I was never able to convince her that money spent for books not absolutely required for the examination was not thrown away.

Needless to say, through Schiller and Goethe my intellectual horizon was extended, the world of my ideas infinitely enriched. But my then incipient weakness for books, so much bewailed by my mother, had another advantage for me, which cannot be overvalued: without it I should never have come to know my father-in-law and my present wife, and I think I have already stated that in that case I should no longer be living.

[1] Translator's note. Philipp Reclam began in 1867 the publication of his "Universal Library," offering the best of the world's literature in tiny unbound volumes at about 5 cents each.

X

I STILL remember just how startled I was when Marie Stark stepped into my room one day, bringing me the Uhland which her father had just bound. She is just my age, and we were then twenty-four. She came without a hat, her dark hair simply parted in the middle; she had brown eyes and wore a blue shawl over her shoulders. Our position in life had a certain similarity, in that I took the place of breadwinner for my mother and she had to act as housekeeper for her father. Her appearance was somewhat womanly even at that time. She looked like a pretty young matron.

I was startled, because I had at that time a quite inexplicable fear of women. Aside from my mother and sister, and not forgetting Aunt Schwab, I had made the acquaintance of neither maid nor matron. Of course I had occasionally exchanged words in shops with proprietress or sales-girl, but that is a matter which alters nothing in the above-mentioned circumstance. Even with harlots I have never had anything to do, less out of chastity than fear. Besides, that was much too expensive anyway.

Marie Stark had a very natural, frank, and unembarrassed manner. I was myself agreeably surprised to see how quickly I was rid of my own fear and constraint. I have forgotten what may have been talked about at this first visit of hers. At any rate, she soon recognized that my foremost care was as much my mother as hers was her father. She fairly idolized her father, as I really almost idolized my mother.

Such were the conditions under which we met.

We also rejoiced at many another common interest, and strangely enough at the fact that neither of us wished to marry, but that we felt ourselves called upon, she to care for her father, I for my mother, till the end of their lives.

WE understood each other, then, and had the impression that we had found each other. And this finding was a stroke of good luck. Two isolated people, alike in age, had met and were enjoying together the happiness of natural comradeship. It became customary for us to discuss with each other the most important matters, i. e., whatever seemed important to us in the care both of our aged charges and of our households. Informal calls on the always good-humored old bookbinder became a habit with me, and Marie too visited me not infrequently.

That mother liked to see Marie Stark come, I doubt. She could not really say anything against the girl, but I assume that she saw as it were a rival in her, that is, she was disquieted by the thought that Marie might take me from her. I know that her plan of life was absolutely based on my remaining single.

My mother clung to me like a drowning person. I often felt this with almost terrifying clearness. She was distrustful of everybody who came near me or preferred any sort of claim on me, not merely of Marie.

The clerk Lorenz Lubota—the sonorous name Lubota is my just heritage from my father—this clerk, then, who limped as if he had a club-foot, and who, when he saw himself in the mirror, could never get an approximately satisfactory impression of himself, was at that time not far from being vain of himself and his value. Besides his mother and Marie Stark, there was still a third woman, Aunt Schwab, whom I have already named several times, who idolized him as a model of virtue.

XII

Before I speak of Aunt Schwab, the only sister
of my mother, it may be well to recall that I
have landed in a quiet haven. Also I will take
a few puffs at my pipe, in order to calm myself
in every respect. It can do no harm to ascertain
that down below, the little shop-bell tinkles
again and again, the evidence of a decent and
honest livelihood. I grafted roses this spring,
painted my seven pear-trees and fourteen apple-
trees with lime, prepared my vegetable garden,
hung up starling-boxes, even put two bee-hives
in operation . . . good, enough of that.

Aunt Schwab, who had a pawn-shop, was
hated by my mother for several reasons. She
had increased tenfold the property inherited from
her father, whereas the fortune of my mother had
been used up in her marriage. A life of work
and care had made my mother poor; a life of
enjoyment, free from care in the main, had made
Aunt Schwab rich. Mother could not forgive
her that.

But mother even thought herself overreached
by her sister in the regulation of their parents'

heritage. In her direst need she urgently begged Aunt Schwab for a loan in order to save her husband from prison, and when the latter at first refused it, she came out with this conviction, which naturally resulted in an embittered wrangle. However, this once Aunt Schwab gave her the money, as I have already said.

The dislike of my mother for my aunt had been considerably intensified by the entire transaction, as also by the debt, which she obviously could not pay off.

My aunt passed far more gentle judgment on my mother, than my mother on her. "She has brought the honest name of Schwab," so my mother would say, "into disgrace and shame as a usurious witch. When one considers that our father was in the city council. . . ." She was surely not wrong, my good mother, in viewing as a decline the development of a councilor's daughter into a pawn-broker. But she called her "usurious witch" and other worse names, pointing to a connection with elements that find a home in thieves' dens and houses of ill fame.

Aunt Schwab's opinion of me and preference for me resembled my mother's. Doubtless she knew what the love of man signifies, but she had never in her life got beyond one or two engagements, and for the rest had remained unmarried. Her business she had always conducted alone, in view of her peculiar talent for figures. After passing the age of forty-five, when small disabilities of old age began to appear, she often needed help, and it was only natural that she should bethink herself of her nephew, whom she could quite justly regard at that time as a painfully honest person.

Now the circumstance that I regularly spent an evening twice a week with Aunt Schwab, in order to chat with her, drink a cup of tea, and at the same time look over her books, once more increased Mother's dislike of aunt, of whom she said that she was capping the climax by trying to rob her of her own blood. But she was on the other hand shrewd enough, too, not to oppose any obstacle to my calls on the supposed testatrix. However, it was not hard to conceal her jealousy and her hatred from her sister, since they had not laid eyes on each other for years.

XIII

THE position which I occupied between the hostile or at least estranged sisters is of decisive importance in that chain of events which led to the dire catastrophe of my life. I saw my aunt with the eyes of my mother and learned to hate and despise her. I saw her with my own eyes and learned to judge her most leniently, to understand her somewhat, but not to love and esteem her. My mother was not wrong in fearing that by becoming involved in her business circles my soul might come to harm.

I graft roses and fruit-trees, bisect worms with my spade, live peaceably with my wife and my father-in-law, have found an inner harmony, a settlement and a conclusion, and am certain of ending my life as a contemplator, without further engaging in a "deed"—deeds dull the wits!—of any sort. We must then take it into the bargain, if Aunt Schwab really does occasionally visit me in my dreams.

XIV

I HAVE hitherto mentioned my own brother and sister only in passing. They are outwardly very different from me. So marked is the difference between us that not even a so-called family resemblance can be ascertained. But my brother and my sister are also outwardly very different. Both are unqualifiedly beautiful, yet the beauty of my brother is more of a delicate and spiritual nature, whereas the charm of my sister consists in a certain primitiveness which is at the same time rather bizarre.

She has the head of a youth. As she wears her hair bobbed, this intensifies the masculine impression she makes. She resembles the head of Praxiteles' Hermes, which is so widely disseminated as a plaster cast. Her neck is very sturdy, her breast broad, but, with your permission, likewise not very womanly. She is slender and firm in build. Her movements are large and free. That her hips are not broad is self-evident, after the above. Her voice is deep, her speech brusque and unconventional. She had great confidence in me, as I have said, whereas my influence upon her was slight. From her fifteenth year she consistently went her own way, which again agreed perfectly with her self-willed, mannish habits. Her name was Melanie, but it did not suit her. She might have been named Konrad, Jungsiegfried, or the like.

My brother Hugo attended the art-school. My nature was much too steady-going, my spirit much too weighed down, to possess in the beginning any appreciation of what he brought home with him from there. The world of artists, of painters and sculptors, remained alien to me at that time. I never looked into it, although an unwearying enthusiasm sought to open it for me.

I had indeed already heard the opinion uttered that he who did not believe in Jesus Christ was lost both here and yonder, in this world and the next, but not, as my brother maintained, that it was the same with those who had no appreciation of the music of a Beethoven, the lyrics of a Hölderlin, the painting of a Rembrandt, or the plastic art of the Greeks.

I was not envious of my brother because he was as handsome as a young god and was smiled at by all the young girls when he passed by, but

I should not have been sorry to be as fortunate, and when he spoke of the power of beauty, which one must feel in order to begin to live, I did not indeed understand him then, but his words gave me food for thought, as the saying is. Long before I really felt the power of beauty, I pondered on it, stimulated by him. He was wont to say, using the words of Christ, but in reference to beauty: "Unless ye be born again, ye cannot enter into the kindom of heaven."

And so I have once more arrived at Veronica Harlan and her wonder-working picture.

In this picture and still more in its original, whom I saw by accident by the whipping-post before the city hall of Breslau, as already recorded, the power of beauty dawned upon me. It dawned upon me in a way and manner of which my dear brother Hugo, the painter, hardly dreamed. A certain Melitta, I said, had given me the picture. Melitta was a girl whom I loved only because a certain resemblance to Veronica endowed her with a faint reflection of Veronica's beauty, so that in her, too, the terrible power of beauty was operative. But enough of Melitta, I shall not anticipate.

I have already written, "So much I think I can say, that when the spark fell upon my soul, a vast pile of fuel had collected in both soul and body." With respect to that spark the question has been asked: divine or devilish? Sufficient if this spark, taken by and large, is equivalent to "power of beauty."

XVI

It was on the 28th of May 1900, at twelve o'clock noon, that I first set eyes on Veronica Harlan and that my destiny thus took its great turn, which might never again be reversed.

I was just coming home that day, and I shall never forget that an inconceivable alteration had taken place there, without there being in fact the slightest change. It seemed to me as if one must perforce stifle in such mole-runs and holes as these narrow corridors and little rooms, although I had lived in them for many years with great contentment. The ill repair of the floor in my room struck me, the spots of mould on the faded, flowered wall-paper, the great cracks in the tile-stove, the ink-blots on the table-top and around the table, the cobwebs in the corners, the lime-twigs black with dead and dying flies, and other things besides.

My condition was incomprehensible and painful even to myself. As when Bottom, the weaver, in "A Midsummer Night's Dream," being turned into an ass, suddenly has a craving for oats, so I seemed to have the fastidious senses of a royal

[34]

being, whose eyes are wont to gloat upon marble and gold. I had the impression of a positively insulting, wholly repellent ugliness.

It hurt me, twice and thrice over, that I likewise got this impression during the usual noon meals in our little kitchen, that I even found my eyes and ears offended by the appearance, the speech, and the behavior of my own dear mother. Fuzz adhered to her venerable grey hair, her teeth were neglected. I felt that she dumped my food before me as if I were one of those creatures that eat out of mangers and troughs. In short, whatever she did, whatever she said, although it was nothing but what she daily said and did, I found myself offended and tortured by every detail.

XVII

THIS manner of seeing and feeling was new to me, and wholly perplexing. It extended to all the daily and common things that came before my eyes in and out of the house. I had perceived something that had now entered my soul, as it were, and was dwelling in it: a something, a sainted image if you will, whereby the lowly and pitiful hut of my soul was transformed into a hallowed cathedral. But this cathedral and this image were now in the wash of an unspeakably base, unspeakably ugly, everyday world, which I had till now really not seen at all.

The highly surcharged state into which I had fallen gave me concern. For although it inwardly renewed and exalted me in an undreamed-of manner, yet I was not unlike a ship that has been torn loose from its safe anchorage. At the same time, my new way of seeing people and things made me unhappy in itself. I knew well that I had previously seen men and things with other eyes and had felt myself in harmony with them. But that was ended; I could now no longer see anything with those lost eyes, or recover that lost harmony. Had I perhaps fallen a victim to some severe psychic disease, which had as it were poisoned the sight of my eyes? Was this disease perhaps even a physical one?

How shall one live in a world in which everything, everything is indifferent or nauseous to him?

XVIII

I HAD such a feeling, as I can clearly recall, as one very likely has after the bite of a serpent, whose poison has made its way into one's body. It circulates in the blood, do what one will to extract it. I had without doubt had a poisonous bite or had been infected by the poison of some disease. One need not die of it by any means; but I could feel that a possibly fatal illness involving unspeakable suffering would infallibly result from it. Should one submit oneself to it with patience, await the possibly infernal crisis in the hope of eventual healing, which was perhaps worse than death?

Some days after the occurrence at the whipping-post, the distraction and derangement of my spirit was so great that several times I barely resisted the violent impulse to throw myself under a passing truck.

XIX

HAD I said this before my judges, they would probably have regarded it as an exaggeration very transparent in its intent. This intent is done away, since I am at most my own judge now and have nothing more to do with other judges, excepting God. But to pull the wool over the eyes of God and myself can not possibly be my intent.

However, I do not say that in my extremity I saw only this one expedient, namely: suicide. I weighed it and inclined to it when at certain moments the thought of hopelessness had united, I might say victoriously, with weariness of life. But the fuel in my soul which the spark had kindled into a fire that now smouldered, now merely crackled, now lifted tongues of flame, but at times burst into a roaring blaze—that displayed countless variegated phenomena which I will describe as well as may be.

XX

EVEN on the very day when I had first seen little Veronica Harlan, and, on arriving at home, was forced to attest the alteration of my visual power, I awaited with impatience the beginning of my duties. The mere walk to the office assuaged the high-strung condition from which I was suffering, because it brought me closer to the spot where I had seen the child. Incidentally, I exchanged at once, and with a positiveness which was not otherwise in keeping with my retiring nature, my seat in the municipal office for that of another clerk, a seat by the window, from which one could keep the whipping-post in view. On one of these days my office chief informed me that an increase in salary had been granted me. This was a recognition of my competence which coming one day earlier, would have transported me into a delirium of happiness. To-day I only half listened. Then three or four days passed before I informed my mother of the fact, which I should formerly have done, most likely, in the selfsame hour.

Of course I did not yet know the girl's name, nor whose daughter she was.

I felt very clearly that in knowing her surname, but especially her given name, I should possess an inestimable treasure, a part of her; that must be balm for my wounds, refreshment for my torturing sensations of hunger and thirst. For as I now saw with terrror, I, an unassuming person who had so far lacked nothing, one might say, that made for a comfortable and modest pursuance of my existence, began to feel the want of the most needful thing of all: light for my eyes, air for my lungs, music for my ears, spring-water and bread. All this could only be granted me graciously by the favor of my indispensable mediator. My state was pitiable.

As I read this over, it sounds high-flown to the last degree. Well, I will by no means maintain that I was at that time a man with a pulse-beat of 58 and a temperature of 95 degrees. Nor should it be thought that I had not tried everything to free myself from the state of dependence into which I had fallen. To the burning mania of all my senses, which craved satiety and revivi-

fication in the girl's presence, I opposed ever a-
new the attempt to satisfy their morbid appetites
in other ways.

In the first days I weighed every possible manner of flight, not only that of suicide. I resolved
to put an end to this with a firm, powerful deci-
sion of my will, and to free myself from the senseless power of this imagination. I did not succeed. Often I thought I had succeeded, when
for example I had spent whole nights cramming
for my teacher's examination, with redoubled
effort in comparison to my former zeal. But ultimately I had always to recognize that the disease had progressed unremittingly, that the fever
had become more intense, the complication more
inextricable.

And so the other possible method of deliverance was once more undertaken. That meant
the attempt to afford these senses, which had now
become awakened and greedy, at least partial satisfaction.

My deliberations were about like this: Try to
get her given name into your power. You will
chew upon it like a cud, and with it quench your
thirst as the desert wanderer, if you like, does

with a stone. You will at all events experience a blissful enjoyment in it, feel it even in your dying, if you should perhaps die of thirst after all. Try to see her, if only from a distance. Stare at her long and ever anew, until she has radiated all her beams upon you, as it were, and squandered them. Then she will have become cold and rayless and can burn you no more. Get at you no more. Or else her rays will continue to stream out, but you will be sated and oversated and therefore hardened to them. Try to speak with her and beg her to take her destructive witchery from you. She must be able to do so since she is herself the witch. Try to secure a picture, a photograph of her, and carry on a cult of mysteries with it behind locked doors. The picture cannot resist your furious kisses, and you can perhaps cool your fires for ever. Seek a confessor: a confidant to whom you can speak openly will take the frightful tension from your breast. You will pour out your heart, and he will take the half of your burden on himself. The invisible beloved will become visible, audible, in short, present, in your spoken words. And the habit of even this presence will perhaps remove the deadly pain of separation. And probably dull by habituation the tormenting need of having the beloved object present.

Unfortunately fear had so driven me back into my own soul that for the first four weeks I betrayed my condition to no one by even so much as a hint. But because I thought that people might detect it from outward appearance, I hesitated to take any steps whatever, however cautious, to find out even the name of the girl.

ABOUT a fortnight had passed, during which my condition showed no improvement. Like a malignant growth which if not cut out spreads and spreads and finally consumes the entire body on which it is parasitic, such was the relation between the terrible and lovely vision and my soul. The actualities about me really no longer existed at all. Breslau had become a city of fantasy, perhaps a Vineta,[1] in which I was in search of a palace of blue turquoise, and the queen of the water-fairies who must surely live there, and from which I only rose under compulsion.

Nobody remarked the change at first, as I did my best to conceal the malady that was couched within me, and successfully played before others the part of my former self.

[1] Translator's note. A once famous Wendish port on the island of Wollin in the Baltic. The destruction of a near-by stronghold by the Northmen (1098) gave rise to the legend that the town had been engulfed by the sea. Sunken rocks in that vicinity are regarded as the ruins of Vineta.

BESIDES, my mother's attention was at that time diverted from my person by vexation and anxiety over my sister Melanie, which she felt more keenly than I. Mother discovered little by little all sorts of things in her drawers and closets which she could not possibly have bought with her wages, she being a maker of flower-wreaths. Long suède gloves, open-work silk stockings, bronze-colored shoes, lace-trimmed shirts, a hat with an ostrich-plume, new and stylish dresses, a new coat, and many other valuables which far exceeded the capacity of her miserable purse.

I had paid little attention to the transformation in my sister, and if I had had my mind on things as of old, I should have taken her seriously to task. As it was, I did indeed support my mother, who feebly appealed to Melanie's conscience, and tried to force her to a confession, and perhaps to a conversion, but with a tolerance towards the possible straying of my sister which visibly astonished my mother. It came to a break between my mother and Melanie, who declared that she was of age and dependent neither on the home nor the support of my mother. And as all this in a certain sense was really true, she ran away and then stayed away, after she had once returned, packed her things, piled them up in a cab, and taken them with her.

Mother spent sleepless nights. She said, "I foresee only too clearly how she will end. She will not spare her old mother the shame of seeing her honest name disgraced, and will at the same time ruin your hard-earned career as teacher. For they do not appoint a teacher whose sister is in the underworld of the same city."

Mother did not dream, thank God, how little impression that apprehension made on me even then.

Strangely enough, I felt myself at this time, so critical for me, more than ever drawn to Father Stark and his daughter. It may have been in consequence of the need of confession which I felt, as already mentioned. Although I did not satisfy the need even here, and though I gave neither the old bookbinder nor his daughter any hint of my experience, yet in their presence I felt enveloped by hearts that loved and understood.

The old man, my present father-in-law—I hear his calm, kindly voice in the shop below—the old man was not only a bookbinder, but he also read many of the books he bound; indeed he himself composed some little stories for calendars. [1] Moreover, people came to him when they needed a bridal or obituary poem, or the like. In the composition of such things he had acquired a certain reputation.

He possesses to this day an almost unlimited quantity of them, and some day perhaps an attractive selection of them can be made.

I wrote my first poem at that time in a manner that is hardly clear to myself. I discovered it, as it were, at the moment when I had written the final period. I shall never forget the joy that was depicted in the face of the old bookbinder when he had read through this poem that I had brought him, and now learned that it was

[1] Translator's note. Annual publications of rather higher type than the Farmer's Almanac, but serving a similar purpose.

born of my pen.　He praised it then in the strongest terms.

"Man, man, why you're a great poetic genius. Here's a fellow squatting in a corner, doing a coolie's work just to buy a crust of bread, and writing things that are worthy of a Goethe and a Schiller."　In this vein my present father-in-law used to talk, and always added, "But now it's time for me to take my own scrawls, this wretched waste paper, and burn it."

XXIII

Upon the supreme critical day, for such was the twenty-eighth of May, followed another equally critical one, which as the sixteenth of June, 1900, deserves to be set down indelibly in the book of my life.

The morning was beautiful, and I had the presumption to indulge myself during the lunch-period in a couple of hot Wieners, which I bought at the entrance to the Schweidnitz Raths-keller, and ate.

At this moment my eyes were directed to the so-called Golden Cup side of the Breslau Ring, about in the region of the large well-known hard-ware-store of Emmo Harlan, whose sign, by the way, I saw continually from my desk in the office.

Suddenly I experienced the utmost consternation. It could not possibly be an illusion—no, what I clearly saw before my eyes could only be the little princess of the whipping-post.

Oh, how I had stared at that post through my window from early till late, as if the girl must suddenly issue forth from it. In fancy I had again and again wreathed that post in roses from top to bottom. I had again and again circled about the post like a fool, without stopping for the scoffing of the passers-by.

This time the enchanting, lovely miracle of beauty was riding in an elegant wicker carriage drawn by two tiny dappled ponies. She had the reins of the little horses in her hand (behind her was a little lackey, beside her sat her governess). She was wearing a picture-hat, and under it was once more the glorious flowing hair which at the very first glance had had such a magically infatuating effect upon me.

If I picture to myself in reverse order, as it were, what took place then, some little exaggeration may creep in; but thereby I shall after all approximate somewhat the state into which I was helplessly thrown on that day. A coachman who was washing an elegant pony-chaise, with his trousers and sleeves rolled up, took the whip which stood in the socket on the box of that same chaise, and cracked it several times loudly before my face.

Only now did I observe where I was standing. In the long courtyard of Emmo Harlan's house, which was overcrowded with scrap-iron, ploughshares, etc., and on which the windows of the salesrooms opened.

The handsome old-fashioned building was known all over town by the name of the Harlan house.

Now it struck me that an elegant gentleman and an elegant lady had appeared in the windows of the second story and had motioned and spoken to someone in the yard.

The place toward which their signs and words had been directed was now empty. It was in front of a little porch, like a church-portal, built of blocks of hewn sandstone.

While they were motioning and speaking, a small wicker carriage stopped before the porch, and an old servant lifted out of it a childlike girl whose face, of the most delicate pink, breathed health, youth, and happiness. She stroked the ponies and let them take sugar from her little white-gloved hands before she disappeared with her governess under the porch.

I was staring after the child when the cracking whip-lash whizzed close by my ear. However, something else must have happened: for why else had so many employees' heads crowded into the windows of the vaulted salesrooms, all staring out at me?

"What do you want, anyway?" a well-dressed young man, probably a clerk, suddenly asked me. "Nothing," I responded somewhat taken aback. "Well, but then why were you running like mad after the young mistress's carriage?"

This second question I answered, to my knowledge, only by a shrug of the shoulders, whereupon I was taken on each side by the arms, and amid general laughter, which seemed to come from everywhere, I was led by two coachmen or porters, not at all brutally, out through the driveway into the Ring, where they left me standing in the stream of traffic.

I think I stood there a long time before I began to move my feet.

THAT morning, that whole day I did not return to the office, although I had an urgent piece of work to finish. Neither did I go home, and I think that for the very first time since she was widowed my mother had to wait dinner and supper for me in vain. It was towards nine o'clock in the morning when my mother saw me again.

All that time I had walked about restlessly, without eating or drinking, for an immense fear had pervaded me when I finally came to myself before the porch of that patrician house. I recognized that here was something which had got me in its power without my will, indeed against my will, and had commanded me.

But if this was so, could not this something, this Daemon which was possessing me, misuse me for still worse things? It was this fear that was calling into the lists all my healthy powers to fight against that Daemon.

I shall remain as cool as possible, and if you like be a little superficial again, in the account of my restless roving, rather than perhaps let my spirit be once more clouded by its confusion, or even entangled in it. First I walked about in the streets and lanes of the city, until I reached the Oder somewhere and followed its banks upstream out of the town.

Even at the beginning of my wanderings my feeling was that I had gone astray and was already far, far away from the familiar and peace-girt spot where I had dwelt in security before the apparition at the whipping-post had entered my life. There is a dream that most people have probably dreamed. On a certain day and at a fixed hour you must be at such and such a place. Very much depends on your being punctual. Unpunctuality, and still more your utter failure to arrive, involves irreparable and painfully severe material and spiritual losses. Never again will that opportunity return, if you miss it. Now, however, this is the torturing course of the dream, that you cannot possibly overcome the incomprehensibly numerous hindrances, in order to reach your destination at the right time: you lack a collar, a shirt, some other important article of clothing, and when you have found one, another has disappeared. If you have finally reached the station in spite of everything, then you have boarded

the wrong train, and suffer the distress of traveling in the opposite direction and withdrawing
farther and farther from the place you wish to
reach. Finally the train may stop, but the door
of your compartment will not open, and before
you can get off, the train is shunted on to a ferry,
perhaps, and you are suddenly in mid-ocean on a
trip around the world from which you can only
hope to return after years. . . . Such roughly
was my condition at the beginning and during
the course of my wandering. It became more
torturing from hour to hour.

XXV

The same Daemon that had misused me for an involuntary and almost unconscious action could not but be that which was now preparing all the hindrances that prevented a return to my old healthy state, taking me with it on extensive aimless labyrinthine paths, and against which I set in motion, alas in vain, all my good angels.

Every thinking person, to the extent of his thinking, is a dramatist. And as I had fallen into a perplexed and tormented state of worry, I had composed in my mind's eye—or it had done itself—a drama of which I was on the one hand a spectator, yet also became involved in its dialogues. Of course the Daemon was on the stage too. And his procedure was so diabolically clever that I, in the most vehement colloquy with him, did not even observe that it was his claw which had meanwhile caught me by the neck and was ceaselessly thrusting me forward with smarting soles and burning brain, together with the entire Thespian cart of my soul, which all the while was engaged in producing its own furious tragic action.

It was the Daemon, it was my mother and Aunt Schwab, and the school-principal Dr. Wohlfeil, whom I had seen on the stage; and the last three were engaged in desperate battle with the Daemon. This Daemon looked like me, to a hair, only that he was dressed in the most foppish fashion: he wore patent-leather shoes and a diamond stick-pin in his necktie. They proved to the Daemon, and I took part in it, that by the illusion of this enchanting little lady of fashion he had planned my destruction. My honesty, my conscientiousness, my lack of pretension, my industry, and my faithful and filial love had been a thorn in his flesh; what he was trying to bring me to was gluttony, avarice, and pride. He wanted by means of an illusion as silly as it was devilish to involve me in folly, madness, and possibly inexpiable guilt.

Enough. I only know that whoso may have met me on this journey, whether it was by day or by night, saw a gesticulating person who talked audibly to himself, and who must be assumed to have escaped from a madhouse.

XXVI

MOTHER was deeply concerned at my failure to appear, but still more at the condition in which I finally came home. She too must have feared the worst for my mental condition. Indeed, I myself thought with horror of a possible death in the madhouse. My fear of it was so great that when mother wanted to fetch a physician I roundly declared that if a physician should enter our apartment, I would jump out of the window.

I slept till the evening of the following day, ate something that mother brought to my bedside, and again slept through until the next morning. When I awoke, I was strengthened and quieted.

Mother had been at the office herself and had adequately explained my absence as due to a sudden attack of illness, so that for this once I had no disadvantage from it.

XXVII

Now there came weeks in which I was almost my old self again. So the crisis must after all have resulted in a success for my side. I purposely avoided thinking back over it. I pretended to myself that I had not seen the apparition at the whipping-post at all, but had only read about it in a book, and that it was about the same with the painful incident in the yard of the patrician house on the Ring. My present wife, then Marie Stark, learned of my mysterious crisis at that time from my mother, as she has recently told me. But both women, with a correct instinct, agreed to make no further allusions to the incident, not to remind me of it in any way. The success which my poem had had with the old master-bookbinder now encouraged me to further poetic ventures, and one day a whole bundle of poems was sent off by Stark to an illustrated weekly in Munich.

What the poems contained and what value they possessed is indifferent here. One verse read for example: "Is't thou, O Muse, that takes me to her service, and like the Sphinx with talons tears the lyric from my breast?" That may sound silly, but it was truly felt. Well, as I have said, the essence and worth of the poems may be debated before another forum. More important to me for the moment is what took place within me after Stark had sent them off to the Munich newspaper.

The strange action to which I was led thereby might have convinced me even then that I had by no means become my old self again.

A glowing ambition, such as had been wholly remote from me hitherto, caused a swarm of provincial illusions, like mushrooms after a mild rain, to shoot up in me. Poems were to me a divine gift, and I did not doubt that since I had condescended to hand them over for compensation, this compensation must be a royal one. Also I assumed, imperceptibly losing the ground from under my feet, that my poetic productions would have a perfectly immense effect and that in consequence my name would suddenly be mentioned with the highest admiration "from the Meuse to the Memel, from the Adige to the

Belt." [1]   To-day it is wholly inexplicable to me
how I could soar to such chimerical heights, but
I yielded to these chimeras so completely that long
before the newspaper had answered I regarded
myself as a rich and honor-crowned poet.

Now since that frightful new vision, that made
everything which I had hitherto accepted with in-
difference appear ugly to me, had not yet died
out again, but had actually directed itself to my
own person and its outward appearance, I stepped
one day in an exalted mood into the leading cloth-
ing-store in Breslau, and actually succeeded, by
posing as a well-known author, in getting them to
note my address and let me walk off with a new,
unpaid-for suit of clothes on my person.

I do not think I was a conscious swindler at
that time.   But with this incomprehensible act
I had taken the first step on the fateful way that
was later on to lead me into prison.

Rejected with thanks, my poems very soon
came back to Master Stark, who, in the extremest
state of moral indignation, thundered out by the
quarter-hour his rage and his contempt of the stu-

[1] Translator's note. A familiar couplet from the national
hymn, "Deutschland, Deutschland über Alles."

pid scribbling rabble, but who could not alter the
fact.   If I assume to-day the opposite case, even
if they had paid for my patchwork verse, still
I could not have paid for a fourth of my mad
purchase with the proceeds.

XXVIII

I MUST now come to Aunt Schwab, which is not possible without a certain effort. In my domestic circle the name is never uttered; I avoid it for my own sake, Father Stark and Marie out of regard for me. After all, she was own sister to my good and beloved mother. And when I think how she met her end, and what part I played in the chain of events that led to her death, I feel each time a wound in my own flesh, with which it is possible to live, strangely enough, in spite of its being incurable.

The quaint little house she lived in was her property. The corner house, you know, between Ketzelohle and Heretic Hill. Her little rooms were handsomely furnished, only somewhat overcrowded with ancient art-objects which she bought and sold, or had kept as unredeemed security. She was not only a connoisseur in such matters, but even had such a liking for the one or the other object that with all her fondness for money it was not to be bought of her.

To spend an evening with Aunt Schwab was not uninteresting, both on her own account and because of the people you could see going in and out of her house. One could make studies of human nature there, and she herself had made them copiously. Aunt Schwab was shrewd, had experienced and seen much, and was perhaps better posted on the scandals of the province, from her own experience, than any other person in town, because high and low entrusted her from time to time with their confidences. For the best-known names of the nobility she evinced not the slightest respect, and I lost mine too when she would draw aside from this or that old family the ostentatious outward draperies they affected. My mother was a simple woman, but Aunt Schwab had a mobile mind and an active thirst for culture. She went to concerts and theatre, and was well posted on the world of music and of actors, and even on politics.

And she was no stranger in still another world, though it is hard to determine whether she herself belonged in it or only touched the fringe of it occasionally. It was the light-shunning world of the crooks. She would often prove to me that thievery infested all classes. She would show me respected men in officers' uniforms, of every mili-

[65]

tary rank, when we were walking the streets together, and would maintain that if someone
should trumpet out only the tenth part of what
she knew about them, they would have to exchange the gleaming coat of the king for a very
different uniform. She named distinguished
ladies who were no whit less clever than the art-
fullest shop-lifters. Some who were married
to the highest personages, mothers of well-
reared children, had the greatest skill in
causing diamonds to disappear unobtrusively
in their suède gloves, in their mouths, or
elsewhere. "I much prefer," aunt would often
say, "to have to do with real crooks than with
folks of that stamp, who will not admit their
rascality in the least. Robbers, forgers, embez-
zlers of trust-funds, countesses and baronesses
that put into their own pockets half of the proceeds from the sales at their booths in charity-
bazaars, consider themselves none the less first and
last as the noblest flower of the nation, and stead-
fastly feel themselves justified in looking down
contemptuously upon their honest and decent fel-
lowmen." Well, who knows how far Aunt
Schwab was right? I think she knew these amat-

eur crooks no less thoroughly than the professionals. These she certainly knew. I have proofs of that which are written as it were with blood and iron into the history of my life.

One of Aunt Schwab's friends was a police commissioner. She declared he had a screw loose, although she had lived on very intimate terms with him, as I believe, for ten years. I am convinced that he had helped her out of many a hole. Really, my aunt and probably the commissioner also belonged in a certain sense in the very group to which Aunt Schwab preferred the real crooks. Convinced without doubt of their civic righteousness, they nevertheless profited not infrequently by goods that had been criminally obtained.

I have met at my aunt's house private detectives, matrimonial agents, inventors of all sorts of patent articles, bankrupt characters of all sorts, theological candidates who had turned into procurers, officers who had degenerated into cardsharpers and been convicted, schoolmasters who had done time in prison on account of moral derelictions, and others besides. I have met there harlots who made upon me the impression

[67]

of decent women, and decent women and daughters of good middle-class houses, who would sell themselves as prostitutes for money with which to pay for furs or a ball-dress, to be worn at a festival, let us say, given by the élite in honor of the Crown Prince, perhaps in the parliament building.

Aunt Schwab, who with her keen understanding had seen through the glittering shell of our social conditions, and perceived the canker-worm at the heart of it, had thereby arrived at a sometimes terrifying open-mindedness. In almost no respect would she deign to recognize accredited values as such. On the other hand, she could almost read off a man's back his character and his debts.

You said yourself, my good aunt, that you had scarcely ever in your life been deluded in this respect. Then I must have been your only delusion. At once your first and last one: for it was a delusion with a fatal issue for you.

She, whose right hand did not trust her left, had conceived a positively criminal, boundless confidence in me; such a foolish, blind confidence that even then I was surprised at it and am

astonished by it to this very day.   How could I
fall so low as to reward such confidence so atro-
ciously?

XXIX

ONE day when I went to Aunt Schwab's, not looking like the same person—"clothes make the man!" [1]—in the suit that I suppose was already the fruit of a swindle, and treated her to the same high-flown expressions about wealth and poetic fame that I had used on the clothes-dealer, she was still so wont to hear from me only the simplest, purest truth that she swallowed the whole thing. She was as unsuspecting as every one else but myself of the poisonous sting that was buried in me and that would not be festered out in any wise. She had not even learned anything of the crisis that had driven me about without ceasing for almost twenty-four hours.

Aunt Schwab was my well-wisher. She was interested in everything whereby my advancement in the world could be promoted. And as she had a high opinion of me, as already noted, my emergence as a poetic genius seemed to confirm her faith in me in an admittedly rather surprising manner.

[1] Translator's note. Both a proverb and the title of a well-known short story by Gottfried Keller.

I told her that a certain Dr. Stark—I was surprised at the ease with which I made a Ph. D. out of the master-bookbinder!—a Dr. Stark, then, having found out about the poems which I had been occasionally tossing off for years, had congratulated me in inimitable terms and prophesied a brilliant future for me. He was just writing an article in which he would make me known as the newly rising star. A paper in Munich would at his instance print some of my poems and had sent me an advance instalment of 500 marks. I can still see how my aunt's eyes grew bigger at these bold impostures. Finally I detected in her a frankly joyful surprise which almost sobered me for a moment. But the fleeting manifestation of my conscience was washed away by the stream of events. My aunt accorded my communications an importance that surprised myself, and immediately fetched a bottle of wine to celebrate the occasion with me.

Now while we were emptying the bottle I observed that I had become an interesting personality to Aunt Schwab, and that she was now surveying me with a sort of timid respect. This alteration flattered me so greatly that I, seized by a sort of megalomania, involved myself more deeply in my web of lies and illusions.

To my horror I recognized that Aunt Schwab had blindly taken on faith even what I had only meant, from my point of view, as a joke. The service of destroying my tissue of falsehoods by a dry jest, such as she had at command on occasion, she seemed for this time wholly unable to render me. Instead of being sobered, I found my intoxication only increased both by her words and the unaccustomed drink. On this day she was of a positively unlawful credulity that was fateful for us both.

So I ventured to yield to the temptation of hinting to her darkly about a matrimonial venture which, as I let her guess, the mysterious Dr. Stark had urged upon me. I had seen the girl, spoken with her parents, had been introduced into the wealthy house by him. Of course my future bride had been won over to me by my poems, as she had given me to understand by word and sign. I finally remarked in passing: it was a pity that for lack of adequate means I was still condemned to an all too modest, all too cautious procedure.

I regarded it as wholly out of the question that this woman, her wits especially sharpened in such matters through her profession, would bite at so crude a bait. But she swallowed it unquestioningly, so that surprise and painful terror made an icy chill run down my back.

On that day I went from my aunt's with a thousand-mark note which she had lent me—a sum that made me dizzy. Till then I had actually never even held such a note in my hands.

XXX

EVERY step in life is fateful, hence I had rather not apply that term to this day, and especially to that step and that second which took me out of aunt's house into the street.

There brooded over the city one of those burning summer nights that are not rare in Breslau.

As I now stepped into the street, I heard my name called by a man who was going into my aunt's house. It was a certain Vigottschinsky, a man of unfailingly neat dress and of youthful appearance, whose age was however not easy to determine. He went in and out at my aunt's, as I knew, and was well liked by her, doubtless by reason of his jolly nature. To this day I do not know the nature of the relation between them. Only this is certain, that obscure business dealings played a part in it.

Vigottschinsky then, for that was the man's name, spoke to me and asked whether my aunt were at home. I said yes and expected that he would go right up to see her. Instead of that he went on to ask, as I was proceeding, whether he might walk a little way with me.

It is not at all clear to me whether he had certain designs upon me even at that time.

Vigottschinsky's manner was engaging, like that of all the Viennese. I must not be surprised if he sought to make my closer acquaintance. Old Miss Schwab always spoke of me in the highest terms, and he was certain that no other than myself would be the rich lady's heir.

XXXI

THESE words, and the entire meeting, affected me not unpleasantly. The false exaltation in my breast had not yet gone stale, and the process of self-deception and self-befuddling was in full swing. It suited me to find a person towards whom I could go on playing the part of a made man.

Vigottschinsky proposed that we should drink a glass of beer in one of the gardens along the promenade.

So there we sat together till midnight, and never wearied of pouring out our hearts to each other.

I have never had any friends, and the pleasure, nay the happiness of such an exchange of confidences was hitherto unknown to me. Moreover, Vigottschinsky was without question a taking personality, whose advances flattered me.

He had taken extensive journeys, knew the great seaports from Hamburg down to Naples, and knew Vienna, Berlin, London, Paris, and Rome. I shall never forget how fascinatingly he could talk.

All told, it was a wonderful summer night beneath the soft rustle of the chestnut-tree tops in the illuminated garden, festively enlivened by gay people, with the lonesome cries of the swans floating over from the city moat. In one of the other gardens near by a band was playing, and the music reached our ears in muffled tones.

Vigottschinsky was really astonished and much interested to learn of my literary bent and my first successes as a poet, which I probably set forth to him in a considerably more fantastic shape than to my aunt. It came out in this connection that he was from my point of view astonishingly well read. From him I heard for the first time the name of Dostoievsky, which from that time on is inseparable from my destiny.

In this night the fantastic structure which I had erected above and around me underwent a marked consolidation.

It was the sweet wound in my soul, the elegant suit I had on, my first friend, the atmosphere of self-deception and false ostentation in which I had this day advanced so successfully at Aunt Schwab's, it was my fancied poetic glory and the faith of my aunt, the faith of Vigottschinsky in

[77]

it, the perfume of strange lands that Vigottschinsky brought with him, it was the summer night,
the wholly unwonted enveloping flood of light
and festivity, the equally unwonted drink, and
by no means least of all the thousand-mark-note
in my pocket—it was all this together that completed my befogging and intoxication.

It is inevitable in such nocturnal sessions that
sooner or later the conversation will turn upon the
relations of the sexes. Of course this is probably
the favorite topic anyway. But in a Breslau
beer-garden, during a hot summer night, it might
only be avoided by one who was blind and a deaf-
mute besides. After all, it is here that the world
of prostitutes and their doubtful hangers-on min-
gles with the populace, and you see the flower of
the city daughters, in their light-colored summer
dresses, and the provocative finery and display
of the local demi-monde, mingling in a motley
throng.

Of course Vigottschinsky and I were also at-
tentive to this throng during our conversation.
We were constantly being attracted by some new
apparition. Vigottschinsky did not dream of
the divine miracle of purity and loveliness with

[78]

which I secretly compared each one of these apparitions, whereupon I hurled them down into Hades.

Vigottschinsky was informally accosted by several magnificent ladies. But he seemed not to be in the requisite mood and to prefer my company to theirs. And they on their part seemed to know him sufficiently to respect his whim.

He spoke very slightingly of them.

Yet by his own account he must have lived the most licentious life.

His accounts were of a shamelessness that frightened me. Orgies in which he had ostensibly participated in houses of ill fame were connected with incidents that can-not be narrated, so absolutely bestial and animal and ruttish.

He must have been positively a frightful scourge to the harlots that he took into his service. And of course that came to light in the court proceedings. That is also revealed in his expenditure of the plunder, which he squandered in a few wild nights.

I never saw him again after the announcement of the sentence. As the king did not exercise his pardoning power, he was executed on a Monday at five o'clock in the morning.

Well, I certainly cut a despicable figure before him as I raved about an unnamed ideal of divine beauty and innocence, the original of which, by the way, I naturally did not betray.

I cannot say that he showed any disdain or scorn in face of my eulogies. Instead he sighed, as I remember very distinctly, and said that if I had the faintest hope of attaining such an object of my love I should be the most fortunate of men. He could no longer count on such bliss. As I view things today, I am astonished that I found it possible, in the presence of the vile and deeply depraved man that his own erotic confessions, even at that time, unquestionably made him appear to be, to lift the veil from a sacred secret even as far as I did, and to respond to his bestial confessions by the prostitution of my spiritual shrine.

Before we went, I changed the thousand-mark note. What I had eaten I could easily have paid for without it. But I could not resist the itching desire to put on airs with my wealth.

The adventures with Aunt Schwab and Vigottschinsky took place before Master Stark had got my poems back. This failure, which he ascribed to the initial blindness of men in the face of everything new and great, was unable either to eradicate my conceit or to sober me in any way.

I felt at some moments, in fact mostly, that something within me must be out of plumb. Once again I was as if in that dream where you see splendid and paradisean landscapes, go strolling among them with rapture and astonishment, and still cannot free yourself of some persistently gnawing torment.

My good mother noticed of course, as she told me later, a marked change in me. I had become silent towards her. I no longer revealed to her, as formerly, all the stirrings of my soul. I went out without saying whither, which I had never done before. As from a great distance I would sometimes see her eyes fixed on me, questioning, thoughtful, distressed, but even such glances had no more power over me.

And those other glances had no power over me, that Marie Stark directed at me in similar spirit.

An instinct told me that I must give her and Master Stark no inkling of the scope of my poetic presumption, and still less of the imagined matrimonial project. They saw that I was altered, that I dressed foppishly and expensively, and that even in my way of life I no longer wished to be the retiring Philistine I had been. I told them that I and Aunt Schwab had plans that were already bringing me in some money, but that would in time bring me a fortune. In a similar way I tried to make plausible to my mother the new lavishness that naturally seemed strange to her.

Even at that time Master Stark and his daughter revealed that trait of character to which I owe my deliverance. One may simply designate it as loyalty. It was based upon an affection for my person which was expressed with equal warmth and constancy by father and daughter. It was motherly in the daughter, fatherly in the old man, and in both it was with a degree of feeling that bears and hopes and understands everything, and is at all times willing to share any sorrow, to shoulder any burden, to make any sacrifice. To be sure, I did not at that time get beyond a vague feeling of the treasure that I possessed in these two people.

I was actually suffering already from an arrogance that made me see in them creatures who were far beneath me, to whom I must condescend.

As for my little municipal post, I very soon found that too beneath my dignity. I was slack in my work and unpunctual besides. When I got a wigging one day on this account, I flared up haughtily and declared that I did not need to wear myself out for starvation-wages in the service of a city that was rolling in wealth. That meant my dismissal.

Nevertheless the affair was finally straightened out by my office chief, who was a well-wisher of mine.

XXXII

I COME now once more to the principal thing, to the idol that I worshipped and that had brought my character and my life to derailment. I still kept struggling against its power, but without being able to escape from its grasp, and yet it tyrannized over me.

Every evening and every morning I wculd promenade around the Ring for at least an hour, back and forth in front of Emmo Harlan's house.

I further attracted attention to myself by buying something in the hardware-store at least every other day.

Once I saw the proprietor going through the store, recognized in him the gentleman whom I had seen at the window, and made him a deep bow.

There were thirty to forty salesmen in the room, and it seemed to me that they were laughing at me. But I did not care.

You cannot know, I thought to myself, how terribly serious this matter is for me, and how I am directed to this threshold by the inexorable finger of God, to find here either life or death.

Laugh! I laugh no less. The courage to live is the courage to die.

Of course I sought in every possible way to meet the little daughter. I knew the times when she drove out, and would always make a deep bow when the little wicker carriage drove past me. The powerful instigation of my Daemon to run after it, as I had done the first time, I was always able to overcome.

However, he betrayed me into other almost equally foolish acts.

When the beautiful child, admired and stared at by everyone, strolled around the promenade with her governess or with her distinguished parents, leading a white greyhound on a red ribbon, I was helplessly impelled to meet her four or five times and to perform each time the ridiculous ceremony of a deeply devoted salution.

It was on a Sunday that I was observed in such a repeated salutation by Vigottschinsky, who then unexpectedly hooked his arm into mine from behind. He frankly confessed that he was now up to my dodges, and he must admit that there was no fault to find with my taste.

Since my secret was now irretrievably betrayed, it would have done little good if I had denied it. So I resolved to be frank, now that I had the confessor I had wanted, and to reveal my passion to its full extent.

I also renewed my lying assertion that I had met with the favor of the beautiful child, and was well liked by her parents. Vigottschinsky hastened to take his oath that this had been evident at the first glance.

Again we went into one of the beer-gardens, this time at midday.

XXXIII

On this day the sluices gave way, and I reveled in pouring out my heart, in the confession of my insane passion. This was a deliverance, a relief that had never hitherto been vouchsafed me. I found or thought I found in Vigottschinsky a man who not only knew how to honor my confidence, but had the deepest understanding of my distress.

I asked him on his conscience whether he thought there was any hope that I might ever possess this creature, without whom I was unable to live. And I was overjoyed when he unconditionally affirmed it.

He then confirmed me in what I already thought I knew, that for me everything depended either on attaining distinction as an author by some lucky stroke, or else on getting a fortune. But the latter was probably the easier and more obvious method, and he would advise me to pursue it.

He mentioned to me a number of cases where a single good idea had made its discoverer a rich man over night. Such ideas he had often had himself, but they had mostly been stolen from him by so-called friends and had brought riches not to him but to them.

After we had eaten, and as we still went on drinking, we fell into an endless building of air-castles, and both of us grew so excited over it that we swore eternal friendship. We stood up, drank solemnly with linked arms, to the astonishment of the people who sat round about us, and even sealed our union with the customary kiss of brotherhood.

Hereupon we shook hands, expressed our joy at having found each other, and mutually pledged our word that neither would undertake anything without the other.

With that our relations had naturally taken on a different aspect. We were now friends, indeed brothers, and could be frank with each other in everything.

Vigottschinsky said, "All right, we are friends, and we want to make money. We want, let's say, to make money by commerce. We must register and advertise a firm, quite unobtrusively if you like. Or we'll simply advertise and not have the firm registered. We'll rent a little office and stock up with some article or other that people are apt to fall for: suppose it's a hair-wash or a mouth-wash or a mineral water. It could just as well be a remedy for debility or a specific to produce a handsome bust, or anything else. Business is business. A real merchant won't shrink from any article that brings in money. We'll advertise and have the money sent in advance. In this way, if all goes well, you get hold of some capital. The advertising section of the newspaper is a keyboard that conjures up ducats instead of music if you know how to play on it. Then when you have the capital, you take maybe two percent of it, have your article manufactured, and ship it out. If the people have to wait a bit, that does no harm."

I made some objections to this.

"Oh shucks," he continued, "every druggist makes a hundred percent profit, and there are absurd earnings in the bank business. Every cigarette-manufacturer wants to get out seventy or eighty percent. In business life you can't be squeamish."

Two thirds of my thousand-mark-note had been spent by this time. I had informed my new

friend of its provenance.   Now when I called to
his attention the fact that advertising itself required some capital, he declared instantly and
without reflection that Aunt Schwab must advance it.

Thus was laid on that day the foundation for
the conspiracy against her to which she fell a
victim.

XXXIV

THE plan seemed at first not so perfidious as it turned out later on. Vigottschinsky knew from me how much influence I had with Aunt Schwab, and I knew that he too had been establishing himself more and more solidly in her confidence. I have already said that I am not wholly clear as to the character of his relations with her.

Well, let us rather say: I am clear.

I spare nobody, because I must serve the truth in this book as best as I can, and besides, there is here no question of good and evil.

I do not pronounce sentence upon myself; how should I do so by others?

Vigottschinsky, who was a cynic through and through, had evoked Aunt Schwab's eroticism, perhaps intentionally, and had left it by no means unused.

So if he and I joined forces against my aunt, we should represent a power over her which she herself had granted us, and for which she was probably no match. And we already had so much confidence in each other as hard-boiled

[91]

knights of industry, that we unreservedly admitted this state of affairs to ourselves and based
our plan of campaign on it.

XXXV

I should be to this day the same diabolical
scoundrel that I must have appeared to be then,
if I had in those days had my feet on the ground.
But the power of Eros had detached me from the
earth and held me fettered in a fixed immaterial
sphere. Hence I can say today with a good conscience that if I did sink into the abyss of crime,
it was due to no really earthly motive and hence
no base one.

To deeds of drunkenness the courts, perhaps
wrongly, allow the familiar mitigating circumstances. A man is not held for the blind and
perhaps bloody deed that he commits in a fever
that is physically proven to have risen to 104 degrees and more. Such a man is not responsible.
Was I at the time responsible?

Such a bewitchingly beautiful child as Veronica Harlan, on the strength of what I could have
confessed as to her influence over me, would have
been taken to the public square in the dark ages
and burned as a witch.

I mean by this to say no more than that the
power of love seemed supernatural in bygone

[93]

days. What do you suppose I should have said to my confessor, in the days of which the wonderful Gothic architecture of the Breslau city hall bears witness, and especially the whipping-post before it, about the influence of the hardware-dealer's daughter over me?

"Your Reverence, I was a peaceful person and I have lost all peace, I was as industrious and assiduous as an ant and now I have become an idler, I was as unexacting as a lame cab-horse and now I have become a libertine and a glutton. I used to love my mother more than anything: if she should die to-day, I should not need to brush away a tear. I used to love God and heaven, and fear the devil and his hell; but tell me to-day where Veronica Harlan is, and though she dwell in hell, I will renounce God and heaven for ever more.

"From the moment when I first saw the girl dates this alteration. I have never touched Veronica's finger, or exchanged so much as a word with her, and yet whether far or near she has absolute power over me. Remote in the flesh, she is nevertheless everywhere present to me. She floats in through my open window by night and glides with equal ease through the thickest wall. She causes me torments which are not readily described, and raptures which can be described no better. She scorches my brain, she burns my liver. She makes me mad. Make the witch take pity on me, or I renounce eternal bliss, and you will cut down my hanged body from the door-post."

After such a confession the Inquisitor would not long have hesitated to deliver Veronica Harlan over to the torture.

Either I had to die, or to find ways and means of winning Veronica Harlan and so securing deliverance. But the ways I had hitherto trod, with and without Vigottschinsky, were of an extravagant nature. That they were in reality not practicable I did not see, because the monstrous illusory power of love had taken from me all sense of the power of reality.

XXXVI

It was fast approaching midnight, and Vigot-tschinsky and I were still sitting harmoniously together and making our plans. Of course we had long ceased to sit in the beer-garden, and had changed our quarters several times. We had gone over from beer to wine, because our confidence in early and large gains rose from minute to minute and I therefore did not need to put any value on saving still further the rest of my thousand-mark-note.

It might have served me as a warning that this day had an excessively strange ending, and in the end not a good one. But I kept seeing nothing but my goal. It was, as we know, a goal in the clouds.

We entered at about half-past eleven a certain centre of night-life, to which Vigottschinsky had introduced me because it was the meeting-place of the handsomest and costliest prostitutes. It was called a café-restaurant, and one could drink in it coffee, either iced or with milk, tea, chocolate, Pilsen beer, every sort of brandy, and every sort of wine up to the best French champagne. Also there were suppers served at many tables.

It was the first time I had ever seen such a genteel harlots' resort, gleaming and sparkling with gilt tapestries, mirrors, and huge chandeliers hung with glass prisms. It is then not to be wondered at if the flood of light, the evening gowns of the ladies, the tuxedos of the gentlemen, the waiters in elegant dress-suits, the dazzling white napery and shirt-fronts, at first intimidated me considerably. I even wondererd for a moment whether they might not show us the door. This was unfortunately not the case.

It did not take twenty minutes to get used to things, and I saw myself being served by a distinguished gentleman in full dress, who treated me like a minister of state.

I was really astonished at the progress I had already made.

Vigottschinsky unobtrusively called my attention to certain rules of propriety to be observed here: that you must not put your knife in your mouth, and that you didn't tap on your glass to call the waiter; but yet he said that nobody could possibly detect that I had not yet mingled in such circles.

I thought of mother and our apartment, and shuddered. I betrayed in my heart simple Master Stark and his daughter, thinking that they were now after all not the right associates for me. Dear father, dear Marie, you have forgiven me for this a thousand times.

Four or five gipsies made with various fiddles and a cembalo some wonderful music, which lulled you as it were into a blissful intoxication. I at once resolved that on this day I should not mind the three hundred marks that I still had in my pocket.

I'll not be shabby here, was my utterly silly reflection, for I am taking my first steps on the parquet-floor of the elegant world, which is also Veronica's world (I had now learned her name and was almost always whispering it).

But perhaps I was not so wrong after all. Among the gentlemen there were those whose distinguished origin could be clearly seen. And it later transpired that even the son of the president of the provincial council was occupying the table in the corner with his ladies.

When I said at the beginning that it was really too bad that we had not been induced in one way or another, directly upon our entrance, to turn around, I was thinking of the experience that awaited me here. There were clouds gathering there for a storm that even in retrospect brings my heart up into my throat.

XXXVII

THERE was a table there in an alcove at which quantities of champagne were being drunk. There were six persons sitting around it, three gentlemen and three ladies. They were excited and never stopped laughing, you might say. Yet although they were in something more than high spirits, their merriment did not for a long time transgress the bounds of what is customary in any decent place.

I noted that Vigottschinsky was in a certain state of agitation and was interested in one of the ladies at that table, who had her back to us. She was a type, he told me, such as he had only once encountered in a young girl, and that had been a Circassian.

I looked that way and was likewise attracted in an indefinable way by the vision, which I only saw from behind. She had something strong and youth-like about her, one might say something Appollonic. But you found yourself thinking that this girl, perhaps not so long ago, might have been riding half-wild horses without saddle or bridle on the steppes of Asia.

We had eaten such a supper as I had hitherto not even dreamed of. Finally Vigottschinsky ordered champagne, though only a German brand, which I of course had to pay for, as well as for a great sea-crab he had ordered. I must now learn to know all these things, he told me.

Engrossed afresh in crab, champagne, chimeras, and everything else imaginable, I had paid no further attention to the table and girl just mentioned, and hence had not remarked what Vigottschinsky suddenly communicated to me as quietly as possible.

He had kept the girl incessantly in view, and claimed to have observed that she had looked around at me several times, and when I tried with the utmost sincerity to talk him out of it, he swore that it was so, and that I could pride myself on the conquest I had made.

I wanted to speak of other things, but he would not desist, saying that there were even stirrings of jealousy at the table in question.

By this time it was probably an hour after midnight. Fresh arrivals hardly came in any more, or if they did, it was gentlemen whose hats were pushed far back, who talked loudly and unceremoniously and whose companions did likewise, or at times even shrieked quite discordantly.

At the tables in the restaurant, too, there was likewise greater freedom and vivacity now.

On the strength of Vigottschinsky's assertions I could hardly help trying to pick up this and that from the conversation at the champagne-table— only there were hardly any but champagne-tables now! And it was really the fact that the Circassian's beautiful wrists, at first only half in jest, were being tightly held by her elegant escort, to prevent her from looking around. Yet she turned her Apolline head on its proud neck far enough around to look me in the face.

Thereupon her partner, the elegant gentleman, was ridiculed by the rest of the table.

A thrill passed through me when she looked at me. But I was so infinitely far from taking any account of an event like this that I gazed quite blankly into the beautiful eyes of the girl; I was indeed smitten by her beauty, wholly strange to me and of a primitive exuberance, but I was still far from taking any further interest in her.

Vigottschinsky and I had studiously continued our conversation. When I looked up after a

[102]

time, the elegant partner of the Circassian had turned his chair half around towards our table and was staring at me with scornful challenge.

People were already beginning to notice the proceedings.

Now the Circassian tried on her gallant what he had vainly tried on her. But she had as little success in drawing him back into the circle as he had had in restoring her exclusive interest to his companions. Then she hit upon the idea of holding her dainty handkerchief before his eyes. Angrily he thrust it aside and rose from his chair with a quick jerk. I can still see how his handsome face, flushed with wine, grew alarmingly grey.

What happened now, and with the speed of lightning, was so surprising to every one, and to me no less, that I cannot recall ever having felt as helpless as I did then.

For before I had made up my mind as to the best way of taking the edge off this most baseless, silly comedy of jealousy, the mad Circassian was suddenly beside me and laughing as she gave me —who had jumped up in alarm—three, four, five, six hearty kisses.

XXXVIII

It will have been guessed whom I had met in this way and at such a place. It was revealed, in a certain sense, that my sister was still the same wilful and independent girl as before, and that she still had her heart in the right place. However, her mad conduct caused me great embarrassment in the fact that I had met her at all in this quarter.

But at any rate our relationship was now cleared up to the satisfaction of her jealous lover, and we, Vigottschinsky and I, were induced to take seats in the alcove with the three couples.

The conversation at their table had all at once grown quite frosty. The spirit of the champagne seemed to have evaporated. The touching reunion of brother and sister made every one thoughtful.

Then too, I must have cut a sorry figure despite my ready-made suit.

And now my sister Melanie, too, had suddenly lost her wild mood, and shrank into her shell in my presence like a schoolgirl. The expression on her face showed embarrassment, almost timidity. My presence seemed for the first time to make her conscious that she had become a demi-mondaine of city-wide repute. This fact I was also having to digest.

She wanted to ask after mother, I could see. She wanted to ask me how I had come by this friend and into this resort. She was ashamed of her company and of her lover, she would have done anything to get rid of them.

No one will be surprised that this group was not exactly pleased with the sudden turn of affairs, which it also felt, and that the one who had caused it was surveyed with rather ill-favored glances.

My situation was certainly of a sort to encourage repentance. And I really had, in this resort and in this circle, as I sat beside my sister, the feeling of being pilloried. I should have liked to steal away unnoticed, or still rather to be herding sheep, perhaps, somewhere in Turkey a thousand miles away. I had the feeling of being leprous, scabious, a pariah, whereas shortly before I had felt as if I were already admitted to full membership in the upper ten thousand. There came upon me, perhaps for the first time in my life, a fury against the class whose sons were brought up with horses and servants, governesses and mistresses, French cookery and costly wines, and could buy with money the body of my sister.

I must have appeared not quite kosher to those around me. I felt dangerous forces rising in me. It was as if my shame were turning every minute more and more into bitterness and silent rage. There was a danger, and it was recognized by my sister, that some sort of kindling spark might fall into my soul and cause an explosion.

My sister recognized too late that it would have been better for her and for me not to have made herself known to me. I told myself, to be sure, that I must make every effort to keep my feelings in check, but I could not prevail upon myself to accept from the lover who was buying her the glass of champagne that he handed to me. Nor could I avoid turning pale in the act, and failing to evade his glance as I had previously done during his fit of jealousy.

Strangely enough, I was also ashamed of Vigottschinsky. I found it natural, and yet it vexed me, that they all edged away from him, as it were, with their looks. The three gentlemen might have been barristers, lieutenants in mufti or something similar. They had waxed mustaches and wore their hair parted in the middle.

Although I had to gulp down a tangle of emotions and thus had enough to do to look after myself, yet I saw that Vigottschinsky was greatly taken aback at the turn of affairs with his Circassian. And I noted that he sought my sister's eye. It flashed through my mind at once that if this went on it might very well give rise to a fresh complication of jealousy. Not long after, however, I also intercepted a strangely searching glance which my sister was directing at Vigottschinsky.

I had been through not a little on this Sunday. My nerves had been played upon violently and unbrokenly, like so many strings, beginning at the encounter with Veronica Harlan and her greyhound, through all the planning and resolving to the oath of friendship, and in the wandering from beer-hall to beer-hall, from wine-room to wine-room.　The meeting with my sister had almost snapped them all in twain.　But now the entire instrument threatened to go to pieces at the slightest additional touch.

XXXIX

Suffice it to say that the danger of a conflict which lay in the tense and sultry atmosphere of that evening was not avoided. I should be reluctant to enter into the description of ugly details. I have spent a beautiful autumn forenoon in my orchard and garden, have shaken my plumtree, and performed all sorts of quiet rustic tasks. How far I am now from the repulsive entanglements of that time, which wound about my feet like hellish brambles because I had my eyes not on the earth, but directed to a divine and distant star. But I will continue my report nevertheless..

All the next day I lay a-bed with a terrible seedy feeling. My deeply dejected, in truth inconsolable, mother nursed me in silence and with a face that seemed to me, when I secretly observed it, to be turned to stone.

Not only because of the shooting pains in my head, which were due to the liquors I had drunk, did she make cold compresses for me, but also because I had a bruise over my left eye.

It resulted from a nocturnal brawl in front of

the Vincent House, and in particular was due to a cowardly and underhanded blow from the fist of my sister's lover.

With that obstinate tenacity which is at times characteristic of the drunken, I tried to induce my sister not to go with her gallant, but to go with me to our mother's. For this I was called by the elegant blackguard the most disgusting names, which would have been appropriate if I had played a part diametrically opposite to my present one, i. e., had accepted money for bringing my sister to him. I was walking along before him in silence with Vigottschinsky, when he suddenly dealt me from behind a tremendous blow on the cheek with the palm of his right hand; that was the beginning of the fight. I am not strong, but I know that the next minute, strangely enough, the villainous, cowardly scoundrel was lying on his back, and that I was kneeling on him with my hands at his throat. As I could not do this indefinitely, and also did not wish to throttle him, I declared myself ready to let him go, on his word of honor that he would keep the peace. This word of honor he solemnly gave me before the whole group, which was still together. Nevertheless, at the very moment when I took my hands away he drove his fist into my face, bellowing; "You damned cur!"

It is a wonder that I did not lose my eye.

XL

I SEE that I have gone into details again after all. Let them stand, although they are without significance for the whole story. It cannot be helped that if you occupy yourself with a matter in any way at all, it will to a certain extent get the mastery over you.

After a relatively short time I had recovered and could pursue the realization of our plans with Vigottschinsky.

My mother had not succeeded in getting out of me what had really taken place the day before, and how I had got into my terrible condition. Nor did she subsequently succeed in wheedling out of me anything about my secret love, nor about my business plans. Vigottschinsky called on me while I was in bed. My mother said she felt a horror of him, and I could see that she was not simply talking.

I calmed her and assured her that she would one day realize what a lucky chance it was for us that I had found this man. He and I debated for a long time as to the manner in which we should wrest from Aunt Schwab the working capital we required; but as to this matter also I left mother completely in the dark.

It may be asked whether the adventure with my sister must not have led to my conversion, whether the blow at my eye must not have waked me out of my terrible dream-life. That was not the case. The condition which I had experienced, and into which I had been cast during the aftermath of my debauch, was really only an intensification of the suffering I had had to endure, every day and every hour since my first sight of little Veronica, in being deprived of her, banished from her presence. Unless I could cherish and foster at least a hope of one day possessing her, life had become a hell to me in any case. Since this hope, which alone kept me alive, could not be nourished by reality—and it certainly could not—it had to go on twining itself about illusions.

Certainly I showed myself a stranger to the world, provincial and without judgment, in finding it possible to believe that a poor municipal clerk, whose sister was a woman of the streets, even if he did secure some little fortune, could have had any success in his suit for the hand of the only daughter of wealthy and respected people; and to that extent my madness did have a very real and very natural foundation.

XLI

THE step which Vigottschinsky and I planned
to take with regard to Aunt Schwab was successful. It is fairly indifferent how we imposed upon
her, and what we made her believe. I have
already told how she had displayed with respect to
my matrimonial project a credulity that was incomprehensible to me, how she had put stock in
my poetic illusions and other chimeras. If I look
for explanations today, I find several. She had
gained her unshakable confidence in me at a time
when I thoroughly justified it. She knew me as
sober and cautious from the assistance I had previously given her in business affairs. She revered
in me a spirit of scrupulous uprightness which to
be sure at the same time disquieted her and caused
her to grant me only a partial insight into her
business.

In the attempt to unravel the entanglements of
deceit, one gets lost in the labyrinth of its eternal
obscurities. So for example I thought that my
aunt was purposely using my unsuspecting honesty to deceive herself and others. Really, she
had formed her judgment of me once for all,

[115]

and had filed the documents away, so to speak. The riddle I now presented she approached from the old standpoint, though it had now become a false one. Besides, my good aunt knew very well that she had sunk below the social plane of her parents. But callouses had formed over this sore spot in her consciousness, and under such circumstances, as is well known, they are doubly thick. Accordingly my aunt thought herself convinced, in spite of all, that she could move in the highest society on equal terms, wherefore she was about as favorably affected by my advance in that direction as one morphium-addict by the confession of another one. After all, my aunt had a true and genuine respect for intellect. Although she unscrupulously exploited to the utmost painters, actors, musicians, singers, young littérateurs, and so on, yet they were the object of her frequently almost idolatrous admiration, whereof an autograph-album which she possessed, with many famous names in it, gave clear evidence. Hence she took it as an accomplished fact when her nephew declared that he would presently move upward into these envied circles, all the more that this would at once be balm to her wound and nourishment to her presumption.

We had then, that is Vigottschinsky and I, coaxed out of my aunt a considerable sum, indeed a substantial capital, with which we established an office in the little furnished room of the Austrian. The fist-fight in front of the Vincent House had broken up the relation between my sister and her lover. I had done my share in this and had met her several times for that purpose. Strange, I had never come so close to my sister before, nor she to me. Only now had I come to understand her, from my eccentric point of view, and by this very alteration in my nature I possessed an attraction for her. She was capable and honest at bottom, and she now threw in her lot with mine again, partly out of a craving for kinship, partly because I had fought and suffered for her. We found pleasure in each other, and enjoyed the unalloyed pleasure of feeling that after so many years of living together we had only just discovered each other.

To be sure, the bond that now united us would hardly have held very long without Vigottschinsky. It was some time before I found this out.

For the moment I suspected nothing when he proposed to take Melanie into our firm, as it were, and turn the clerical work over to her. Of course I knew that she could make better progress with her pen than I or my brother Hugo.

Our office was a long slit with a single window from which one looked down at the entrance to the Lobe Theatre. Vigottschinsky's bed stood in it, and there was just room enough to squeeze past it in reaching the desk, which stood by the window. The room had old dark wallpaper, which hung down in spots. Moreover it was high and hence quite sinister.

Four weeks passed in conferences in this room. These conferences were however nothing more than objectless chatter, which was spiced with immoderate drinking and smoking, and which became a pleasure that we sought again and again.

Objectless chatter is perhaps not a fitting expression, because it did not indeed turn on actual and sensible objects, but so much the more on imaginary and senseless ones. These have the strongest power of attraction for worthless people.

Air-castle-builders and idlers of every sort know that. My sister was a permanent member of that company.

At that time I had strangely arrived at the settled conviction that I had succeeded in the moral redemption of my sister, in lifting her out of the dens of vice. I was so blinded as to see a further piece of good luck in Vigottschinsky's liking for her, especially since it was returned and had led to an engagement. This engagement, a marriage, what could be better adapted to win back my sister to the ranks of honest citizens?

It was astonishing to see the power that Vigottschinsky had gained over the beautiful girl. Her self-will, her upright nature, her contradictory spirit were as if blotted out. I had long since had to form suspicions of the nature of the relations that connected my sister and my friend. But I had too much to contend with in myself, and both Vigottschinsky and Melanie left nothing undone to make their relation appear like a serious, straightforward, and lawful one.

In the Lobe Theatre they were playing evening after evening, "Around the world in eighty days." Towards nine o'clock they regularly executed on the stage a surprise attack by Indians, whose shots one could plainly hear in our room. Our longing to travel, to roam through the wide world, was of course always freshly excited by this. We dreamed of adventures, fairy lands, and riches. In this and other ways time was squandered and money wasted, without our making a beginning at any business, reliable or unreliable.

I had resigned my post in the municipal office as soon as I had the money from my aunt in my pocket. However, it was not quite easy to take leave of my place by the window of the city hall, because that meant giving up my view of the whipping-post as well. To my office chief I had little by little conveyed a fairy-tale concerning the change in my fortunes, in which, quite seriously, a rich marriage and incipient literary fame were alternately stressed more or less. But the strangest part of all was that I believed the fairy-tale myself.

XLII

So we were merchants now and had to put on a good social front. It was not possible to do business without that. Vigottschinsky very soon cut quite a good figure, although he did not spend on his outfit half as much as I. They say that people with a hump-back, or with a limp like me, not infrequently have the inclination to trick themselves out in a ridiculous fashion. I too fell a prey to this inclination. I thought I owed it to my business, to my importance as author, and to the idol of my love, to make a complete dandy of myself.

So I bought myself white collars and expensive linen, four or five stylish suits, patent leathers, gloves, cravats, hats, provided myself with a stick-pin, cuff-buttons, and a gold watch, and when I was thus togged out and in my silk-lined summer overcoat was striding up and down Schweidnitz Street, I never passed a show-window without mirroring my idolized person in it.

It goes without saying that we also used my aunt's capital on every possible occasion to give ourselves a good time. Every day we went to beer-halls and beer-gardens, and sometimes to those unpretentious wine-rooms that can be found in Breslau.

It would be a mistake to assume that I did anything at this or at any time without reference to my absurd goal. The picture of Veronica Harlan—not the one that lies before me, but the imaginary one—did not leave me for an instant, nor the thought of it. Of course she is in truth the epitome of sweetest loveliness, and was still more so in the intoxicating exhalations of my soul. Always I stood under the spell of a constraint that completely enslaved me, but at the same time turned my slavery into ecstasy. But at the heart of this ecstasy dwelt pain and despair.

XLIII

I LOOK back upon my completed existence from a distant, lofty, secure position. I survey the path, the network of roads, and the landscape from which a happy exit was finally found after all. The Lorenz Lubota of today, whom father-in-law and wife call Lenz, has made the Lorenz Lubota of the past the object of his meditation. Lenz! They call me Lenz! Well, why not? Is not every spring [*Lenz* is a word for spring. Tr.] preceded by the stormy November, the dark December, the ice- and snow-bound January, in short by autumn and winter? Perhaps they are not so far wrong in this appellation, if it is to suggest new sprouts and the blossoms of future fruits. Is there not growing up here perhaps, under the calm strokes of my pen, a fruit? Is the air of my spirit not pregnant with sprouts and strange blossoms? To be sure, this spring that I am living through to-day is nothing compared with the one that in those days passed over my soul, with its warm showers, fantastic blooms, burning suns, and delirious tempests, when we were engaged in squandering the gold of our first plunder. Exuberant raptures like those of that day have never since swelled my breast to bursting, but to be sure no more pains have harrowed it such as were then my daily bread. For it should by no means be thought that my then condition was nothing but sheer rapture. I had rather the feeling that blood was being sucked out of my heart by some great spider day and night. Hence I have written, as I see in paging these leaves, that a pain was the innermost core of all the raptures I felt. And that pain was very great.

What can be more terrible than to show to a thirst-parched throat the mirage of the coolest spring? A morbid, lying, deceptive certainty, whereby the voice of hopelessness has been buried and violently silenced. What can be more painful than the occasional waking of the sleepwalker, even though he succeed in saving himself from a plunge into the depths by clinging to the eaves-trough? Can a man who is fundamentally honest completely forget that he is so, and put his conscience to death? I at least never had the feeling of guiltlessness when I was running through my aunt's money, even though I did not exactly let the feeling of guilt rise in me. I mostly used to gulp down the dainties of the restaurants like so much gall and poison, even though I did not know it outwardly. Besides, I was so to speak gutted by a terrible passion. A conflagration raged within me. I could have cried out to my judges that all my insane commissions and omissions came down to nothing more than the attempt to put out this ravaging fire. I could have proved it to them, or else I may possibly succeed in doing it with this memoir. I could have wished to throw myself under the wheels of an omnibus, I have somewhere said. Not once, I may add, but countless times did I think of that. I also considered putting an end to myself by drowning in the Oder, or with the bullet or the rope.

But from all this I was restrained by the thought that I should thereby leave the earth on which Veronica was living.

I do not conceal from myself that if I had attained the presumptuous goal I then sought, the plane of happiness secured by it would have been a very different and much higher one than that plane upon which I can stand to-day in peace of soul. Earthly rapture would then have attained to a supernatural degree and would have perhaps been unendurable to a mere mortal in its all-overshadowing, blinding splendor. I confess that in spite of being wholly cheerful and content in my peaceful little circle, I have in this respect not made a full renunciation. Only I have transferred all fulfilments of that sort into the "better life."

XLIV

I COME now to that point which was one of the most momentous in my complicated course of error, self-deception, megalomania, and crime. In order to get it as clear as possible, I discussed it all thoroughly only yesterday with my father-in-law, as if unintentionally, sitting in the arbor over a glass of beer. The good old man knows that I am working on the story of my fall from grace, a belated argument for the defence which is to teach my judges to understand and to pardon; for to understand all means to pardon all.

Stark still regards me to this day, as in the time of our first meeting, as the great writer of the future.

There can be nothing pleasanter, nothing more comfortable, than our evenings in the summer-house. Yesterday it was especially fine. My Marie of the simple goodness, with the heart of purest gold, had prepared for us, as always, the most delicious supper, consisting of eggs, cheese, sour milk, and fresh bread and butter. The insects buzzed, roses, elders, and honeysuckle scented the air, also the firs on the edge of the near-by woods. Though it had grown dark, the air had not lost its body-heat. The monstrous disk of the moon hung behind the elders and larches along the village brook. The murmur sounded doubly loud in the nightly stillness, in which not a twig was stirring. Fireflies gleamed in the grass of the round common.

Marie had gone back into the house when I began to speak of my hare-brained suit for the hand of Veronica Harlan.

But I will tell it as it happened.

I had learned that the lovely girl was betrothed, indeed that she would be married in a few days. Vigottschinsky had got the information. That was of course wholly absurd. But just as on the one hand my hope grasped at every straw, so the most improbable rumors were capable of casting me into a boiling maelstrom of torment. In short, I was aflame with jealousy.

Veronica was at that time, I judged, about fourteen. But I might have been deceived, she might perhaps be between fifteen and sixteen. Why should a sixteen-year-old girl not marry?

And what might not and could not be possible and usual in her enviable circle?

And so I composed that letter to the father of the child, hardware-merchant and recently appointed kommerzienrat, [1] a letter which to this day is beyond my comprehension.

I could not help it, I had to write the letter. It was as if somebody else guided my hand. But always when I spoke of this circumstance, or said anything about Veronica, I mean during my trial, I was told that they were not interested in that, that it had nothing whatever to do with the case. Strange enough that when one is to pass judgment on the guilt or innocence of an accused, the essential motivating or exonerating factor is not included in the scope of the cross-examination.

"What are your letters to us?" they said. "Write as many letters as you will, we don't care about them, unless they contain incriminating or exonerating matter with respect to the crime that has been committed."

My letter to Mr. Harlan was grandiloquent and bumptious.

[1] Translator's note. "Councilor of Commerce," an honorary title bestowed on successful financiers and business men.

[129]

How was it possible, how could the letter of a fundamentally so timorous, so modest, nay even so sober a man as I, who had a pimply complexion and a limp, was imperfectly developed owing to lack of nourishment in his youth, and was repulsively ugly according to his own conviction, turn out so impudent and arrogant? It must have been that in my character, as you might say, not one stone was left upon another.

"To this day I blush with shame," I confessed to my father-in-law, "when I think of that inexplicable letter."

For I had declared in it that I could in no case consent to the betrothal, and still less the marriage, of Veronica Harlan to any other than myself.

Thereupon my father-in-law said, "Why shouldn't the letter have been dictated to you by some evil Daemon that had an interest in putting you in a hole?"

I have forgotten to say that my father-in-law had been an active spiritualist, many years before we knew each other, and that during that time he had been in active occult communication with his deceased wife and many other spirits. When we became acquainted, he had already given up the practice of table-tipping and in fact all active spiritualism. Marie had little inclination for it, and he himself had lost with advancing years that passionate curiosity about the life beyond. However, he possesses a work, "Manuscripts by Spirit Hands," bound by himself in forty handsome volumes, which is unique in the world and may perhaps some day attain universal significance as a storehouse of unheard-of revelations from the fourth dimension. I myself do not go near it.

Who should be surprised if I got no answer to my hare-brained letter? It is well known that the rich not infrequently get letters from insane people. No one pays any attention to them. They are thrown into the waste-basket.

At that time, however, it was far from my thoughts to make clear to myself this natural state of the case, and more and more I enveloped myself in the narcotic exhalation of my megalomania.

Is it credible? My presumption had taken an enormous leap upward since I had written to the rich hardware merchant. The bold and resolute letter to this patrician gave me by reaction a feeling of social equality. I carried my head much higher than hitherto, and floated in a stupefying sea of conceit. I thought to myself, as I walked through the streets and the passers-by streamed past me: I hope you are not unaware that I have written a very serious message to Mr. Emmo Harlan to tell him of the bone I have to pick with him. Yes, I know he did not answer. From that very fact you can see the effect my letter had.

I told myself in quite sober earnest, as it seemed to me, that the silence of the great merchant was a good sign for me. The answer to a letter like mine must be considered from every angle. The breaking-off of the previous engagement could not be done rapidly, and then too they would probably institute inquiries with respect to my person. But in my megalomania—I had been told, by the way, that the poet Byron had also had a club-foot!—I did not doubt that I should be described to the Harlan family as the rising star in the poetic firmament.

XLV

ONE day while I was thus waiting, I was again possessed by what my father-in-law had called an evil Daemon. I had just vainly asked the postman once more about the expected letter, when I ran straight home to change my clothes and to get myself up with a solicitude which I must at present characterize as absolutely ridiculous. And the result was ridiculous, too. I might easily have read that in the looks that followed me with ironical astonishment.

I took a cab and gave the driver a definite address—you will guess which one.

The whole thing went with such lightning speed as I had really not ventured to hope for. I had assumed the title of Doctor on my calling-cards. The servant to whom I gave the card disappeared with it in the inner apartments. He returned, and I was ushered into a blue salon. I had to wait a moment, and it was nearly eleven o'clock in the morning before the beautiful Mrs. Harlan rustled into the salon. She immediately stopped short, as if she had expected some one else, and declared, recovering her composure directly, that that had indeed been the fact. She had been expecting a Doctor von Trota, a young assessor and a friend of her brother. Then she said, "But what do you wish? I presume you would like to see my husband."

I answered with a trace of timidity that that might not be necessary as yet.

Mrs. Harlan looked searchingly at me. She may have noticed that I was only keeping my composure with an effort. I felt, but could not help it, that there were twitchings around my lips, that a hard lump was squeezing my throat, and that hot tears were coming into my eyes.

"What is your pleasure, Doctor?" she said then.

But suddenly she bethought herself and cried, as if she had now guessed the reason for my coming, "Of course, of course, take a seat! I had almost forgotten that we have advertised for a tutor for our Veronica. I am surely not mistaken in the assumption that your call is connected with that."

I thought of my pedagogical leanings and my studies.

For reply I said, "No, dear madam, the days

[134]

in which I should have accepted a mere tutorship are forever past."

I myself was somewhat taken aback when this strange answer had escaped me. I felt such a giddiness as if I had leaped across an abyss, but was still unable to get a firm footing on the other side after my foolhardy leap. And in other ways my answer did not satisfy me. If I had only not put in that word "mere."

"Do you consider a position as tutor to a young and talented child something so insignificant?" Mrs. Harlan naturally rejoined with astonished mien.

Then I vigorously pulled myself together and said how gladly I should certainly accept such a position if I had not taken the liberty of calling about a different, far more important, and far more serious matter.

I had now reached the outermost tip of the rocky promontory, from which there was nothing but a leap into empty space.

XLVI

Today I am sober and in perfect health. All the more I must say to myself that that person, who was then in the house of the hardware-merchant as suitor for his daughter's hand, was a sick man. Why, it is impossible for me today even to understand my conduct at that time. There are crises of growth, crises of puberty, which are an inevitable and, as it were, healthy malady. It may perhaps have been such a so-called children's disease, some kind of infection.

My feeling at that time, even when I was facing the beautiful Mrs. Harlan, was that I should not act as I was acting, had I not lost a certain inhibiting power over certain forces of my soul.

My conduct was that of a high-flyer, unless it was that of a lunatic.

I come to that part of my speech, and of my general conduct at that hour of irresponsibility in the house of the hardware-merchant, that has remained fixed in my memory.

"Dear madam," I said, "it would be a very special honor to me to act as tutor to your daughter, if my destiny and the hand of God had not directed me to far higher goals and especially one higher goal. My father was a staff-officer"—the green tax-collector's uniform of my father gave me this idea!—"my education most careful. From childhood on I have received plain indications of every sort, that pointed to a great future career for me. I should not wish to appear boastful, but I may be permitted to inform you of the fact that this coming autumn a drama of mine, 'Konradin von Hohenstaufen,' is to be performed in the local municipal theatre. A great scholar whom I will not name, and who possesses the largest library in Breslau"—I was thinking of my present father-in-law, the Master Bookbinder Stark—"has designated this work as perhaps the greatest since Friedrich Schiller.

"I am well-to-do, dear madam. How else could I have ventured on this step? My financial assets are invested in safe securities. Also I am a partner in a well-inaugurated commission-business, but to be sure only nominally, since my ideal inclinations and aptitudes disqualify me for a strictly commercial career. Dear madam, as a genius I stand to be sure at the beginning of a long and thorny path. But I hope to be worthy of my talents and to endure to the end the divinely ordained martyrdom"—I hastily added—"of the great poet and thinker. I am resigned to the mockery, the misunderstanding, nay even the blindness of my fellow-men, for did not a far loftier than I not shrink from the path to Golgotha? Permit me then, dear madam, to present myself as the author of that letter which your husband doubtless received about two weeks ago. The writer says that he has an older claim, a higher claim to the hand of your daughter than any other, and goes on seriously to prefer his suit. Be assured, dear madam, that I am most sacredly in earnest in this matter."

XLVII

I DO not know where I may have picked up all these well-turned phrases. They came from my lips as smooth as butter and without the least hesitation. And this is certain: while I was speaking I believed what I said.

Just by the mere sight of the mother of Veronica, my idol, I was lifted up above the real solid ground of real things.

Yet it was of course an incredibly injudicious act to involve myself in so coarse a web of lies, which could so easily be torn asunder by anyone but myself. Across the way was the office in which I had worked for my mother and her children as a poor starveling. A step to the police-station would be sufficient to determine exactly what was my origin and my general situation. But in the exalted state in which I was, with the fear which impelled me and the splendor that was luring me on, the thought of being unmasked was as far from me as from a man with the best conscience in the world.

Mrs. Harlan had listened attentively to me. It seemed to me several times as if she were looking hastily about her, as though seeking aid. When I had said everything, as I thought, and was waiting in expectant silence, she rose, went to the wall, and seemed about to ring an electric bell. As she did so she said, "Your proposal, sir, is very honorable." Then she added in effect that her daughter was to be sure still a mere child, and too young to marry. But, all in good time, for today she would say neither yes nor no.

While she was saying this and other things like it, a servant came in and soon after Mr. Harlan himself.

Harlan was slender, carefully and even elegantly dressed, and had trinkets of coral on his gold watch-chain. I immediately resolved to buy myself watch-charms of the same kind. And I subsequently did so, but of course they took away from me all my finery—not that I am shedding any tears over them—as goods stolen from my aunt. Mr. Harlan entered, and his wife, as I distinctly observed, winked at him as she informed him of the subject of our conversation.

XLVIII

Before I again stepped into the cab that was waiting for me before the driveway of the Harlan house, I could not forego standing still and letting my eyes stray over the Ring, while I slowly buttoned my kid gloves. My conceit, or rather my self-deception, and my folly had reached their highest point. In my own eyes I had achieved a fabulous success. Today I know, of course, why Mr. Harlan acted and had to act, as he did, as if he were agreeing completely to my proposal. He simply took me to be what I was. And because it is dangerous to arouse a lunatic, the best thing to do is to give him no occasion for contradiction.

Upon my persistent urging the following questions had been discussed before I went: whether I might see and speak with Veronica, whether I might write to her, and how long they wished to postpone the marriage. "I propose," said Harlan lightly, "that we let three months elapse before you speak to my daughter. I shall regard it as unnecessary that you should correspond with her for the present. After the lapse of that time we can see whether your affection has remained constant.   But we must positively allow my little Veronica," he ended, "two years for her development before she is led to the altar."

My present belief is that my courtship was regarded in the Harlan house as a welcome jest, and was thoroughly and heartily laughed at.

For me, to be sure, it was more than a jest.

I was ready to burst with pride and presumption as I stood there, still unable to decide to step into the closed cab.   I looked up at the windows of the Harlans' house, in the hope of catching sight of my beloved.   To a fellow-employee from the city hall, who noticed me and bowed, I paid no attention.   I saw my present father-in-law, the worthy grey-beard, being led by Marie—he needed that support on account of his weak eyes —approaching on the sidewalk.   The kind people discovered me.   Marie blushed to her eyes with happiness, and the old man, on being acquainted by her, at once waved his handkerchief at me with a merry smile.   But to keep company with them now seemed to me wholly beneath my dignity, and so I jumped into the cab in a sort of flight.

"Drive me to Hansen's restaurant," I ordered the driver.

XLIX

Several days have passed during which I have
not written any of these recollections of mine.
Well, there is no hurry. The weather has been
fine, and I could take beautiful walks, or I might
better say journeys, to Erdmannsdorf, through
the old park of Buchwald, and over to town or the
little Schmiedeberg. My family can run the
little shop and the little farm, with its few chick-
ens and several goats, almost without my help,
and they like me to have all the leisure I can. As
an experienced clerk, the book-keeping and the
correspondence of our little business cost me little
time and effort. I can do that with my left hand,
so to speak.

I purposely wanted to pause and reflect for a
few days, really to divert my thoughts, before
I proceed to render myself an account of my momentous relations with Melitta.

The little one was sitting with her mother, the
so-called baroness, at a side-table in that same
fashionable restaurant which I had named to the
cabby before I got into his cab, probably chiefly
for the sake of impressing the passers-by.

You will recall the excited condition into which I had got myself after leaving the Harlans' house.

In reality I was astonished and had to bethink myself a little, as the cab actually stood still before the plate glass windows of Hansen's restaurant.

Even Vigottschinsky had never ventured into this most fashionable and most famous restaurant in town.

As for me, such a step had been heretofore the very last thing to be thought of, because I had never yet got rid of my vague feeling of being an outcast. Suddenly I had got into this Eldorado of all epicures, without knowing how.

I do think that for the first moments I conducted myself fairly well; but I had difficulty in facing the glances of the guests without confusion. To the left of the entrance of the long restaurant were sitting cadets and officers of the royal Breslau cuirassiers. Handsome men, tall, slender figures, rich, aristocratic lads, every one of them belonging to some noble old family. They had the condescension, it seemed, to stoop to this resort, which common people were also allowed to frequent. The other tables showed faces of men mostly of mature age, which simply could not fail to inspire respect. Surely many of them, physicians, professors, city councilors, bore the most resounding names in town. I distinctly heard someone called Your Highness. Yes, and there was sitting in a discreet alcove in the uniform of a general, in distinguished isolation, the Duke of Ratibor, who as commandant of Breslau was a well-known figure. Somehow too I thought of police and presiding judges and similar high officials, in the light of several glances whose cross-fire I had to stand. No, it was no enviable moment when I stepped into that restaurant, and I should not care to live through it again.

It should have brought me to my senses.

And in the presence of all these persons of rank I actually did come to my senses, in a way. But when I had been shown with exquisite politeness to a table all by myself, and had sat down at it, I found myself reassured by the thought of having enough money in my pocket to pay my bill, and of owing it to nobody in this circle, but at most to my aunt. And besides, I was a free man and no longer a clerk at the city's mercy.

Quite certainly, however, it was a strange thing that a little despised starveling could dine table to table with the highest officials of the city, the province, nay even of the state, as like to like, and not be shown the door.

Now whether it was to give myself courage, or to put myself in the proper light here at the outset, or in my treacherous feeling of triumph—anyway, I immediately ordered champagne.

Certainly, the luxury of the fashionable world includes exquisite enjoyments. It is after all not surprising if one who has learned to know them, and then has to give them up, turns criminal for the sake of them. This was probably the case with Vigottschinsky. Unbridled sensuality possessed this man, talented in his way, and even attractive in many respects, and destroyed him. This danger is overcome in me.

The nourishing soup, the delicious fish, the fragrant roast, the game, the dessert, and last but not least the excessively luscious wine, put me into a very satisfied mood. The artificial light, which has to burn all the time, even by day, in that restaurant, except just in front of the single plate-glass window, added to its cosiness. Then there is also the darkening veil of the clouds of smoke, which to a certain degree isolates the individual guests and even yourself. You seem to yourself to be in a hidden cave, in a hiding-place, and you feel as if you could sin with less interference. After I had sat there half an hour, I felt as if I had been taken into a secret society in which everyone wished his neighbor every joy.

L

MELITTA was sitting, as I already said, with her mother at a sidetable. The girl had a little lap-dog that wore a tiny bell on its neck. When Melitta let the lap-dog down on to the floor, its leash reached just far enough for it to rest its dainty little fore-paws on my left thigh. Of course I made friends with it.

The baroness thanked me several times with a faint smile for this friendliness. Once she reproved Melitta in an amiably reproachful tone, because the gentleman—that was I—was constantly being annoyed by her dog.

Then Melitta looked around at me.

At the sight of her face a sort of terror must have shone through my expression, visible to the baroness. I saw how she lifted her eyebrows, as if in question.

And I was actually frightened, because Melitta to my thinking resembled Veronica in a remarkable way.

From this moment a wonderful confusion began in me, whereby in a mystic, or let us rather say abnormal, manner I united the images of the two girls.

To be sure, I told myself, this girl is not really Veronica, but Veronica is giving me a sign through her, is using her to get into communication with me.

This idea took shape like a flash and possessed me from then on like a perception of the highest truth.

Melitta seemed to be Veronica's age. I found out later, to be sure, that she was considerably older, but still I could never really convince myself of it. Now whether it was her clothes, or whether her growth had been retarded, she had for me something absolutely childlike. She wore Veronica's loose blond hair, falling in glorious long waves. Her eyes were brown, her dainty little nose was tilted the least little bit at the very tip. And the way she moved that tip, when she spoke with what I might call the mouth of a suckling, had an especial charm for me.

It was evident that she was the object of conversation at the table of the cuirassiers. But however the looks of the gentlemen strayed over the table of the baroness, the little one seemed insensible of them, and one could clearly see that she returned none of them.

On the other hand, she did reveal an outspoken interest in me, strange to say.

This fact surprised me on the one hand, but was at once brought into connection with my new fixed idea, whereby it was made to seem, on the other hand, not particularly remarkable. My mania, which was giving me the delusion of a supernatural concatenation, turned the striking behavior of the child toward me into something that was quite as it should be. And only that, I mean my mystical conception of the matter, gave me the courage to follow it up.

To anticipate at once: Melitta had a real affection for me. I have a number of proofs of that. How that was possible in my case, who up to the time of my great crisis had never really ventured to count on such an experience, is uncertain. I did indeed have my simple and even sober friendship with Marie, but at that time it was not to be mistaken for passionate love either on my side or on hers.

Nor did the affection of Melitta for me ever rise, I suppose, to the height of such a passion. Yet for this girl there could be nothing in which love, and indeed a very actual love, did not have a part.

LI

I will put together certain traits which I have arrived at by reflection and which make somewhat comprehensible the affection of Melitta for me.

She was the strangest specimen of the genus Woman, I suppose, that there could ever be in the world: outwardly a childish school-girl, inwardly of unswerving, mannish independence. This independence was the same both in thinking and in acting. All attempts to break it down—they had often enough been made by her mother—always led merely to the same failure.

Never, she declared, would she let her right to love be starved. She told her mother to her face, with great calm and firmness, that she intended to deny herself absolutely nothing in this regard. If a man pleased her and the opportunity could be found at all, she would take him. She had not the least intention of going out of the world, without once having enjoyed, and enjoyed to the full, the best thing in life. If anyone tried to prevent her, let him look out for himself. Whoever did that would be her enemy.

It was natural to hate one's enemies. But she was capable of a deadly hatred of that person who should try to rob her of the greatest good in life, that is, of nothing less than life itself.

Nor did Melitta merely uphold such views with her tongue: her mother could tell a tale or two about that.

As I know from my own trial, the visits of the lawyers, the physicians, and the clergyman in the prison, and from my own private reading in my cell, there is such a thing as perversity. Melitta had perverse leanings. So she would often say: she had rather die than have anything to do with one of those dandified dolls, the officers of the royal cuirassiers. Here her repugnance, her utter aversion set in, whereas an ugly and probably filthy old fellow could make a strong impression on her. The baroness told me that she had for a long time given herself quite un- reservedly to a shock-haired, gout-racked, greasy old cabaret-actor.

So perhaps the way in which Melitta swooped down upon me at first sight, as they say, is to be ascribed to perversity.

To be sure there may also have been involved

in it some sign-language between mother and daughter, with reference to the snaring of simpletons. A free life was the prevalent practice with them, without disagreement, only that the mother wished to spend it in a well-considered, well-applied, purposeful manner, whereas this was a secondary consideration for the daughter.

Well, all one, even through my narcotic fog I perceived what manner of persons I had run into the arms of. And after the dog had given rise to an informal conversation, I quietly made bold to settle the ladies' bill together with my own.

I do not know how they had found out about this circumstance, but at any rate they rose soon after, to leave the restaurant in silence, with a significant, suggestive smile and a nod of the head at me.

Needless to say that in two minutes I too was on the street and at their side.

LII

ONE can imagine how complicated my circumstances had become when in less than twenty-four hours—Melitta hardly gave me that much time—I had entered into a fixed liaison with her. The sweet and utterly depraved child was my preceptress in the art of love. As my aunt had put the capital expressly into my hands and not into those of Vigottschinsky, I gave him substantial amounts of it, but kept the lion's share [1] for myself. This melted away at a furious pace.

As I did not wish to betray my relations with Melitta to Vigottschinsky and my sister, yet they could not help seeing that an estrangement had come between us, I was again forced to take refuge in lying. It was perhaps a good thing that Vigottschinsky's sagacity soon got on my trail and thus took this burden off me. He took it as a matter of course that I too had now given up my narrow-minded ideas about love and had proceeded to action.

As for him, the investigation later on showed

[1] Translator's note. The lion's share (see Æsop) was the whole. Hauptmann seems to have fallen into a common error.

that excesses of every sort had become second nature to him. At that time, although his relations with my sister were just at their zenith, he managed just the same to find time for deceiving her with other women. My sister did not dream of this at first, but later he no longer made a secret of it. His shameless frankness, however, only seemed to intensify her love. At least she acceded to his lightest wish with a doglike servility.

When I recovered my sister in that night-resort, her conduct as compared with formerly had become finer, even ladylike. It was Vigott-schinsky who really made a harlot of her.

He carried photographs around with him, mostly unspeakably vile little ones in series, which disgusted me, and would spread them out before us with cynical laughter. He had got them from sailors, he said, who had brought them along from Port Said or other international dens of vice. His speech teemed with obscenities. He never thought of taking my sister any more to resorts like the one in which we had found her. Instead he dragged her around among the very meanest gin-shops, where women waited on table, and where the dregs of humanity gave itself up to the beastliest orgies. Before I came to know Melitta, he and I had taken several, I suppose, of those so-called beer-journeys by night from one ale-house to another, but never without my being thoroughly ashamed of myself afterward in consideration of my ideal, Veronica.

LIII

HAD I not been so taken up by my affair with Melitta, I might perhaps have prevented Vigott-schinsky from dragging my sister so completely down to destruction with him. Left alone with her, the scoundrel had an easy time of it in this regard. In the first weeks I did not dream of the obscure, subterranean ways that he was wont to walk with her. When in the blackest night of my life I recognized how deep she had sunk, a horror came upon me, as I distinctly recall. I saw no reason why I should have failed to observe through what a terrible school she had meanwhile been taken by that blackguard. What had become of my sister, frivolous indeed and all-too-hungry for life, but fundamentally always straight and outspoken and strong of will?

He dragged her with him through every gutter and puddle, through every rubbish-pile and gar-bage-heap. He introduced her into his circles, those of the obscurest of all "men of honor," and domiciled her there, sold her favors or used them as his stakes in three-card monte. And if the poor girl ever rebelled, his fists broke her resist-

ance. Finally she had lost all power of rebel-
lion, as the force of vice had completed her
subjugation. She could no longer do without the
smell of fusel brandy, the rowdyish delirium, the
bestial enjoyments of the vice-dens. Before
the crime against Aunt Schwab was committed,
nay even before it was planned, she had already
"turned a trick" [1] now and then, as the rogues'
cant puts it, and this came out in the subsequent
investigation. She confessed to me that several
times she had had to lure gentlemen into definite
quarters, so that Vigottschinsky's political parti-
sans—he draped his basest crimes with the mantle
of politics—could the more easily rob them.
She had stagged [2] and furnished other kinds of
mechanical assistance in all sorts of crimes.

I must not anticipate and not digress.

The day on which I had made my insane
marriage-proposal in the Harlans' house, had
subsequently dined and drunk champagne in
Hansen's restaurant, and had finally been taken
home with the baroness and her daughter, to
awake the following morning in Melitta's arms

[1] Translator's note. To carry out a theft.
[2] Translator's note. Thieves' cant: to stand sentry.

—that day, I say, had not only torn me completely loose from the solid ground of my former life, but had finally silenced the voice of reason within me. From now on I lived in a world which no longer had the slightest element in common with that in which I had formerly existed. Indeed, it had nothing in common with any real world. I confess, however, that it was full of new and intoxicating sensations, and that it conjured up about me unspeakably glorious phantasmagoria.

LIV

I HAVE just been paging through my manu-
script and feel that it is time to speak again of my
poor, honest mother.

I was still inhabiting my old little room, that is
I still used it to sleep in. But to be sure very
irregularly in every respect, as I mostly came
home towards morning and spent some entire
nights every week in the apartment of the baroness.

My mother still had towards me the respectful
attitude that was based on my former exemplary
life. She still saw or wanted to see in me the
good son, the rock on which she could confidently
erect the secure asylum of her old age.

Of Veronica Harlan she knew nothing, of
Melitta as little, as she had no social intercourse,
hardly ever stepped over the door-sill, and only
ran the most indispensable errands to the baker
or butcher, or into the nearest dry-goods store.
Marie, my present wife, visited her now and then.
But neither Marie nor her father knew at that
time any more about me than my mother did.

The disappointments of my mother's life had

caused her to shun the world. She never went to see other people, and when Marie or perhaps her neighbor across the corridor succeeded in disturbing her in her hiding-place, she never disavowed her preference for seclusion. Even if there had been people who knew about everything that I was doing, and if they had told her, she would not have believed it, indeed she would in all probability have rebuffed even the attempt to make such a revelation.

The transformation which she observed in me, and which she could not explain to herself, she interpreted as sickness, I am certain of that. Hence it never occurred to her to lecture me on moral grounds. She seemed to be totally incapable of that, as far as I was concerned. She always merely cast troubled looks at me, and I evaded them when I could, since they were the only thing that made me uncertain in what might be called my ecstatic gymnastics on the tightrope.

My mother is dead. It was grief that put her under the sod. I am certain of that, although the physician told me for my consolation that she had lived her life out to its furthest limit. Her organs were worn out, the examination had disclosed. But what have I said as to the part played by grief as a grave-digger? It was not grief nor worn-out organs, it was the pitiless and brutal blows that destiny dealt her heart which caused her death.

And I may say that I never returned to the old dwelling without feeling that I was going into a mouldering grave. I could just as well call it a coffin. It was the coffin in which, as it seemed to me then, I lay buried alive for many long and horrible years.

LV

My mother, I said, took me to be sick. After her death they brought to me in prison a letter which had been found in the drawer of her sewing-table. It was very long and addressed to me.

It transpired from this letter that she had for a time thought me demented, but hoped that I would some day recover and be wholly myself again. She had experienced something similar many years before with one of her brothers.

The baroness and her daughter sucked the life-blood out of me. The girl was without doubt a consumptive. Either she infected me, or else, which is more probable, I had likewise been carrying the germs of that disease in my system. At any rate, I was in the hospital during almost the entire period of the trial, since I took to my bed shortly after my arrest with pulmonary catarrh and a fever of 104 degrees.

Melitta always had a slight fever, probably without knowing it. I suppose that caused the shine in her eyes, the purple patches on her cheeks, and her burning, insatiable mouth.

From this malady and this internal fever probably arose also her blazing, unquenchable sensuality, which made her favors as intoxicating as they were depraving. She had completely enslaved me.

Melitta ate little, and never any meat. She neither drank nor smoked; otherwise, she said, the fine sensitivity of her nerves would be blunted, which involved for her the highest delights of life. What self-denial with so much lack of moderation! And yet she was good and said she loved me because I was so good.

Melitta asserted that she would soon die. She is living to-day, but has disappeared from Breslau. They say she went somewhere in the South. Some said that a rich Brazilian had traveled after her for a long time and had hanged himself on the door-knob of her hotel-room, because she remained cold to him. The fact was that she liked almost anybody. Age, class, or other advantages or defects made no difference. The red coats, it is true, were repulsive to her, and when she disliked somebody, she disliked him, and he got nowhere with her, even though he squandered millions over night.

Let no one think that I reveled in the possession of her in a simple, natural manner. As I have said, the thought of Veronica and her image did not forsake me even in Melitta's arms. We have lain awake in close embrace for entire nights, and it not infrequently happened that I would dissolve in sentimental tears and confess to Melitta the cause of my unhappiness. She expressed anything but jealousy. She rather clasped me the more wildly and tenderly. "I do not love happy people," she said, "I love only the unhappy ones. The more you suffer, the more ardently I yearn to comfort you. If it does you good and eases your pain," she would often say, "then close your eyes and imagine that you are holding the other in your embrace."

She did not know the delusion that always enraptured and tormented me in her embrace: namely that in some way she was a greeting, a part, a mystic emissary of Veronica Harlan.

Towards the end of the summer Vigottschinsky and I had to meet for a conference. The money of my aunt was spent, and we had to decide how we should coax more out of her. Such an attempt was not easy.

For a long time we were of two minds as to

[167]

the sum to be extorted, of which each of us this time was to administer (as Vigottschinsky called it) exactly one half, for he insisted on that. As I needed him and feared I might otherwise lose his aid—I felt that he had me in his power to some extent with respect to my aunt—I had to consent to this arrangement. He proposed a sum that was twice and three times the one we had squandered.

I still remained timid, although I needed the money more than he did, since I had paid all sorts of large and small bills for the baroness and her daughter, and had even got into debt. Gold ornaments which I had bought for the little one I had already had to pawn secretly to Aunt Schwab, as if I had got them from a friend. The baroness gave me to understand, Melitta never, that I was either solvent, and then I must prove it with clinking coin, or else, as she ironically put it, I must seek out another sphere of action. She must live, must provide for her daughter, think of her future, and besides—nothing for nothing.

We had given up in our private talks the fiction that we were still trying to get business capital. This was strange in view of my general high-flown airs. I probably viewed this matter so dispassionately because the knife was at my throat. I could detect that my friend had previously only pretended that he believed in my poetic fame and my matrimonial prospects. What I had done and attained in the meantime made me appear in his eyes less idiotic than artful. He left me in no doubt of this. But I had no desire to initiate him into my mysteries.

I have already spoken of the social cloak in which he liked to drape himself. He had continued to perform certain services for Aunt Schwab, even though less consistently, and gave me to understand that in this way he could withdraw from the entire affair, if he chose, and leave me in the lurch. But all the same he hated my aunt. I was horrified to see in what an implacable form this came to light while we were forging our new plans. But he draped his social cloak about this too.

My accomplice declared that he was an anarchist, and that he approved of any and every means of depriving the bourgeoisie of their plunder. He had vowed war to the knife against the exploiting state, against capitalism. Property was robbery, he maintained, and there was the greatest merit in robbing a band of thieves. If one theft succeeded, then at least for once justice would be satisfied in detail and in particular.

But now especially one must regard women like Aunt Schwab as cancerous sores on the body of humankind. He called her a blood-sucker, called her an old hyena, who lay in wait for those mortally wounded in the social struggle and fell upon their dying bodies, in order to fatten on their carrion. And he called her a disgusting old vulture, who stank of her nauseating trade a mile away and sat in her dwelling like that carcass-eating bird among the clean-picked bones of a fallen beef.

So tremendous was Vigottschinsky's hatred, so immoderate and wild his fury, that I was unfortunately carried along into its maelstrom to a certain degree—remember the hatred and despite that my mother felt towards her sister.

So then the new swindle was thought out between us to the last detail, and fully "planted," as the phrase is.

LVI

To be brief, this stroke succeeded too.

It could only succeed because the usurious old witch, as mother called her, had still not lost her blind confidence in me. To be sure, we had gone to work with unexampled cunning, too. Vigottschinsky's liaison with my sister and his tenacious plans with regard to my person had caused him to utilize his intimacy with my aunt in confirming her confidence in my honesty, my caution, my business judgment. And he had also undertaken to prepare her for the coming blood-letting simply by a shrewdly devised fabric of lies with respect to my business successes and by admiring eulogies of my character. It is honestly true that we subsequently sat over our wine and laughed like fools at this base and scoundrelly trick, and especially at the role of demi-god which he had had me play, while he had depreciated himself in every way and even left himself out of the reckoning, in order to give more weight to me.

We got from Aunt Schwab a certain hundred-per-cent-earning industrial stock, which I promised her that she would get back untouched, as

I merely wished to deposit it at my bank as security, and for three months at the most.

In less than six weeks this new money had run off through the same channels as before, and we were just about to plan another stroke, come what might, when Aunt Schwab all at once awoke from her pipe-dream.

One day I came home and learned that she had been at my mother's. It was the first time in a decade that this had happened. I cannot say what took place then between the two estranged sisters. I did indeed find my mother pale and agitated and with trembling lips; but she would not give me any disclosure of importance. She merely fixed upon me her old, grieved, and sadly questioning glance, perhaps with less timidity than usual.

In a letter she had left behind my aunt asked me to come to her.

Now there did come over me a sort of realization, which increased to consternation.

I had already been living during the last weeks as if under the pressure of an ever more darkly lowering cloud. Moments of clearness showed me to what dangerous cliffs and precipices I had rashly climbed. The burden of my cares grew and oppressed me. I not infrequently cried out in the night and awoke bathed in perspiration. I sought consolation in religion and felt springing up in me the desire to be able to renounce the world, to spend the rest of my days behind the walls of a monastery. I was a Protestant and considered conversion to Catholicism, since the old spacious Roman church seemed the most likely to afford me an asylum. A deep weariness came over me. It was a weariness of life of the sort that craves nothing but rest and peace, and fears any resurrection as merely a new hardship. I had at this time already laid out Veronica's body in my heart like a beautiful corpse. My soul was as it were draped in black. The catafalque stood in the midst of it, covered with flowers, and with lighted candles around it. But the room seemed to derive its light not from the candles, but from the unearthly glory of the beauty of my dead beloved. With this image in my soul I wanted to go out like a candle, and as I have said with no anticipation of a resurrection. Of course there were other moods, too. When less exhausted physically, I had supermundane hopes that burst through my surfeit of life. I saw myself then in the sphere of Veronica, who had become a seraph, and God had allowed me to feast myself to all eternity solely on the splendor of her beauty.

In my first consternation I went to look for Vigottschinsky. We considered what was to be done.

First we must find out how much information my aunt had of our doings, or whether she perhaps had only a vague suspicion. Hence we were agreed that I must take the disagreeable step of going to Aunt Schwab without delay. "For," said my pretty friend, as he urged me to haste in noticeable anxiety, "she would be capable, in her first alarm, of turning us over to the prosecutor without a word."

LVII

Aunt Schwab had opened the door for me herself when the faint tinkle of the tinny bell had died away. She did not speak to me, and let me step into her parlor in silence.

The red plush sofa squeaked as she sat down on it.

Now I spoke my first "Good evening," and asked, for it was already growing dark, whether I should light the lamp.

But there was no answer. Nor did my aunt ask me to take a seat.

A dray rumbled over the pavement of Heretic Hill. The canary in the adjoining room, a triller from the Harz, made a last effort to offer the setting sun his customary tribute of song. My aunt still said not a word.

"You sent for me," I stammered, "what for?"

Still it seemed not to be a part of my Aunt's plan to reply to me, until after some time she finally made up her mind.

Whereupon she said these words distinctly and clearly with a firm voice: "Lorenz, you are the most contemptible scoundrel I ever knew in my life."

At these surprising words I felt as if the knife of a surgeon had split me open from the throat past the navel and down through all my intestines to the backbone. Never in my life have I felt a pain like it.

LVIII

It is good to pause a little, to light my chilled pipe again, to step to the open window, to listen to the finches and red-breasts, and to tell myself where I am, before I go on with my confessions.

I have now done that to the full. I have saluted the doctor, who drove by on the street in his new one-horse rig—he has a good practice, he can afford it—I have listened to the talk of the children who are bringing berries and mushrooms which they want to sell in the shop below. And I have breathed in the odor of my cabbage-roses, which comes up to me out of the front garden. This has quieted my heart-beat. It means a great deal to me to be clear-headed and cool as I descend into the deepest and most dangerous shafts of my life, into their infernal passages and mazes, where deadly poisons float about in the mine-gas. Can there be a greater miracle than that I am now enjoying once more the light of a golden day?

LIX

So Aunt Schwab, sitting in the dim light on her red plush sofa and looking up at me, her idolized nephew, had said these words: "You are the most contemptible scoundrel I ever knew in my life." And I, as I have just written, felt myself exposed to the backbone by a single slash.

At this moment I was confirmed in the realization that I was indeed no longer worthy of Veronica and must treat her as one dead.

Yet my heart cried out for her in this terrible hour, in which the death-blow was being delivered to my moral personality. Yes, I should have died blissful, with the exultation of any Christian martyr, if I might have made her understand, lying at her feet, that like a moth I had sought and found death in her flame.

Later on I once yielded to the inward impulse to reveal this to the beautiful child, who had never even so much as exchanged a word with me. The letter came back unopened.

There can be no thought, however, of trying to describe the storm that arose in me at my aunt's words. It is certain that before I allowed the first word of my answer to escape from my lips I had regained my composure.

I felt the whole seriousness of my situation, and was resolved to leave no means untried to avoid being unmasked.

The direct and excessively brutal attack of my aunt afforded a basis for my defensive tactics.

"First let me light up," I said, and proceeded to do so without undue haste. Then I continued, "There, now we have light, and now we'll look at everything in the light."

"You know I am no friend of excitement," said I, as she was about to burst forth. "If I really am what you say, then our getting excited won't change it, either. By the way, I am thirsty," I had the impudence to conclude, "for you know I don't like to keep you waiting when you send for me, so I've been hurrying. Perhaps you might give me a bottle of beer."

She began again; "Lorenz, you are the most contemptible scoun . . ."

"Don't take any more trouble at all," I interrupted her, "for I pay no attention to anything that has no basis in reason, and if you are going to continue like that, don't be surprised if I reach for my hat. An hour will surely come when you are in a better humor."

She managed to pant, "You two have deceived me, give an accounting." She wept. She could not get out another word.

I said calmly, "Who has betrayed you? What 'you two' do you mean?"

Of course the details of the conversation are no longer in my memory. At any rate, I knew ultimately beyond a doubt that my aunt, probably through her police commissioner, was pretty well informed about our actions.

I had succeeded, or at least I thought so, in making plausible to her a certain business connection between myself and the baroness, because the latter could be very servicable as an agent. The liaison with her daughter was denied and roundly declared to be a base calumny. Likewise Vigottschinsky's liaison with my sister, as that infuriated my aunt more than anything. At the same time I gave her to understand, or at least pretended to, that I did not approve of her own relations with Vigottschinsky. The mere fact that I knew of them embarrassed her. I was only acting along his own line when I tried to strengthen my aunt's confidence in me by expressing my doubts of Vigottschinsky's character. I went further and said that his name could not possibly be registered as partner in the new firm. So much had become clear to me by listening here and there, I said, that the decent commercial world would absolutely reject him. At times it seemed as if by such subterfuges my aunt could be made to change her mind again after all, and be won over to renewed confidence and even to an apology. I got my beer after a time, yes and had to share her supper. But I kept feeling all the time that the peace was deceptive.

The speech to which she adhered was about as follows: "I may have used too strong an expression when I called you a scoundrel. It may be that I have been misled by gossip and calumniation, and that the business you are doing promises profit. Today is Wednesday. You have till Saturday. Either Melanie and you will appear Saturday noon at twelve o'clock with all the accounts of your business, or you can count on sitting behind iron bars with your accomplices on the evening of that same day. Let the baroness look out for herself too."

LX

UNTIL daybreak Vigottschinsky, my sister, and I held a council of war in our so-called office, with wine and cigars. At about half-past nine we heard as usual, from inside the theatre, the blank cartridges of the great Indian attack. The great theatrical hit, "Around the world in eighty days," was still being played. The ground was rather hot under us, and we should have been glad to set sail for the new world, or anywhere else.

Our situation was fairly hopeless. Not because we had no account books. We did not think that my aunt would immediately deliver us over to the courts on that account. First of all Vigottschinsky would try to make another of his attempts at reconciliation, and then too my aunt had reasons for being very reluctant to have dealings with the courts. No, our case was hopeless because we had contracted other debts and absolutely needed more money, without any prospect of squeezing a single additional red cent out of Aunt Schwab.

This state of affairs did not seem to find Vigottschinsky unprepared; but for a long time I did not know where to turn. I thought of stringing myself up, but I could not even think the thought of crawling back into my cast-off skin. Rather die than admit before Melitta and her mother so pitiful a downfall. And anyway: I could die and thus be torn from Melitta. But I was incapable of tearing myself away from her while living, from the enjoyments and ecstasies that she knew how to give. No, if the worst came to the worst, I should perhaps end it all by a leap into the Oder. Vigottschinsky, as I say, seemed to have reckoned on the present crisis and to be closer to his goal. He favored my aunt with the filthiest expressions, which outdid anything that his hatred had ever achieved in this direction before, and spared no means of egging me on to a like hatred of her. I had reported to him verbally the sentence which my aunt had used to greet me with, and this sentence, in which I was branded as the most contemptible scoundrel, was indeed well suited to awaken in me the desire for retaliation, and, put to good account, to cause a wild feeling of revenge to flare up in my deranged mind.

LXI

I DID not see Melitta or my mother on the following day; for my sister, Vigottschinsky, and I did not lose sight of each other. Without its being said, I felt that there was something wholly new and fearful between us, whereby we were being welded together in an unexampled manner. It seemed quite natural to me that we should breakfast in an out-of-the-way basement lunch, that we took our dinner in an ill-lighted den which bordered on a disreputable, tumble-down tenement, that we drank Nordhausen corn-whiskey with it and at evening were still drinking corn-whiskey, and that we stayed awake all that following night, or at most slept a little in our clothes, our arms resting on a pot-house table, our foreheads pillowed on the backs of our hands.

In all that I had so far seen and done in these two nights and a day I was helpless, in the main. We were drifting as it were on a resistlessly flowing stream. Vigottschinsky steered our craft. Whither was he steering it, what goal had he chosen for the journey? A vague presentiment of it may well have breathed upon me, much as when you go past some old bit of masonry, and from a basement hole the chill iron and mould-laden breath of a subterranean torture-chamber makes your soul shudder.

I lacked any power to take the rudder from the helmsman. Or to jump out of the boat. Either death awaited me in the flood, or in spite of my attempted flight I should in the end be drawn alive into the wake of the boat and so be carried along to its fearful goal.

The subsequent testimony of Vigottschinsky decidedly contested my passivity: I had frequently behaved wildly, and by furious pounding on the table had at times deadened his doubts and his conscience. I denied this before the judge. But if I really did so, then probably the unwonted and immoderate consumption of brandy took from me any recollection of it. I have since attempted countless times over to recall to my memory those fearful nights that preceded the crime, and truly it may be a fact that I made on him at times the described impression. One and another trace of it rises dimly in my memory. But in that case I behaved noisily in order to disguise my inward weakness, my lack of the "will to the deed." Perhaps I willed the crime without wishing it, and thought in my wretchedness that I could keep my hands clean if I let Vigottschinsky's plans take their course.

Upon these nights followed another day. On the night of Friday we were going to proceed to the execution. In these three nights, without any exaggeration, my hair turned gray.

Even on the evening before the deed, which was carried out without me, I was wholly apathetic. I had become acquainted with all sorts of types of male and also female rogues, and had plunged with a kind of suicidal fury into the vortex of sensual orgies. Things went on there, and my sister even participated in them, than which nothing more animal or satanic can be imagined, and the recollection of which still corrodes my soul with burning stains. Inextinguishable, stinking stains.

When I took leave of Vigottschinsky on the evening before the crime, after we had agreed on the hour and place where he was to pass the plunder on to me for his greater security, I hoped that the unendurable tension in my brain would soon degenerate into madness. And when instead of this I subsequently recovered my senses in a prison cell, that too was a great blessing to me.

My aunt was to be robbed. The scrapp [1] had been framed by a practised peter-man, a rascally friend of Vigottschinsky, the latter, my sister, and myself. I use these terms of the rogues' cant because they became familiar to me in those fearful nights. The rogues had even initiated me into their guild with a grotesque dance and a baptism of corn-whiskey under the name of Crookleg. In the opinion of the experts the "scrapp" could be managed without difficulty. The only thing was not to have just the worst kind of bad luck.

Of course there was no idea of even touching a hair of the victim's head.

The whole affair went off exactly in accordance with the predetermined plan. Only unfortunately it was overstepped in one single point, which to be sure cost Vigottschinsky his life.

Vigottschinsky visited my aunt on the basis of his former but now somewhat cooled relations,

---

[1] Translator's note. Thieves' cant. Scrapp=plan of robbery; frame=to prepare; peter=a safe; peter-man=safe-cracker.

to which however, in case he seriously wanted to do so, he knew how to give the old warmth. He was bringing my aunt good news. There was awaiting her, he said, in the visit of myself and my sister on the following day a great satisfaction.

Aunt kept him to supper, as was to be expected, they drank some wine, and so it continued according to programme, in that she kept the rascal with her over night. The latter had put a sleeping-draught into her last glass of wine just before going to bed, and in view of his position of trust near her, it was easy for him, even if she should awake, to hold her attention and to divert her from the proceedings in the adjoining little pawn-office. It was a feature of the general depravity in the nature of Vigottschinsky, that his sensual impulses shrank from nothing when it was a question of his advantage.

From midnight on my sister had to "stag" on Coppersmith Street in the rain. Various "high-balls," that is signs, in which she possessed a great skill, had been agreed upon for the approaching "peter-man." Also she was a past-mistress, as her darkness-loving fellow-rogues said, in the arts by which one manages to divert any disturbance that threatens, and to entice the disturber away from the scene of action. I am convinced that the fabric of the plan was of long preparation, for everything was so ingeniously thought out and with so many precautions.

Soon after twelve Vigottschinsky opened a window, and when the watchman had passed on his rounds, he threw down on the pavement for my sister, as soon as she stepped out of the shadow of a certain gateway, the house-key carefully wrapped up in paper. Melanie picked up the key and walked, at ·first slowly, then faster as soon as she had turned into a side-alley, on a definite, long, labyrinthine course, leading to a pre-arranged spot where she handed the key over to the "peter-man." He now set out for my aunt's house, whither she followed him, but at so great a distance that she could just barely keep him in sight. She walked into Coppersmith Street at the very instant when the rogue disappeared in my aunt's house.

LXII

I HAVE often wondered why Vigottschinsky did not want to carry out without me his unquestionably long-cherished plan. He was better acquainted with my aunt's habits than I. He knew exactly where she kept her cash, certain valuable papers, and her jewelry, also where she hid the keys to all these special receptacles. He had made my aunt's house the object of his close scrutiny in the course of several years, and knew his way about in it better than she did. And if he could not manage the mechanism of the fire-proof safe, I certainly could not do anything for him, so much the less that my aunt never let anyone come near that steel fortress. So he could not do without the cracksman and other accomplices of the rogues' guild.

Well then: what use had he for me, to whom he must after all turn over a goodly portion of the plunder, if all went well? I presume, in the first place, in order to stiffen his own back, since he was probably only a beginner in the profession of thief. Out of the honesty and stability which he saw in me he made himself the firm prop, the post that he needed, in order to let the creepers of his criminal ideas twine around it. Welcome to him was moreover my combination of ingenuousness and folly. Such a fool as I, if rightly used, one might perhaps be able to employ as a dummy, or to pull the chestnuts out of the fire. And then it would ultimately not be hard to cheat him out of them again, without even having burned one's own little finger. Then let him perish, covered with burns. But who can genuinely illuminate the fine and complex motives of the soul? Of course there are often quite inactive persons who are only capable of developing their energy by making common cause with others. And who knows but that Vigottschinsky just simply had a fellow feeling for me.

The plunder was to be handed over by the cracksman, since Vigottschinsky did not wish to leave the house, partly to my "stagging" sister, partly to a certain reliable man who was to set off with it to Dresden that same night. My sister, on the other hand, was awaited at the Freiburg station by a so-called officer's widow, who was traveling with her son and who was to receive unobtrusively my sister's part of the plunder and carry it to Berlin. The place and date of the so-called "smack," that is, the division of the spoils, had been fixed in a little town, upon the punctual observance of which one could rely without any danger of defalcation, according to Vigottschinsky's assurance, in view of the honesty of the thieves among themselves.

Vigottschinsky believed himself capable of watching the discovery of the burglary, on awaking the next morning, of simulating horror and astonishment, comforting my aunt, and encouraging her in the hope of recovering the stolen goods, of notifying the police, and taking the first steps for the discovery of the thieves. I am convinced that his impudence was equal to this plan.

In that night cash and other valuables to the amount of at least one hundred and twenty thousand marks were stolen by burglary from the pawn-shop of Helen Schwab. Of this entire plunder very little, on the whole, was ever seen again, perhaps a gold ring, or a gold watch with a monogram. This success, however, which did no good to either Vigottschinsky or me, was only secured by a hair's breadth.

At the door of the old house of which the pawn-broker occupied the second story there was a bell-pull by which one could even get her out at night. It was hers to decide whether she regarded the money-seeking night-hawk both as deserving of confidence and as a sufficiently juicy morsel to make her open the door for him. Such a night-hawk my sister had successfully intercepted and lured into a dark alley by means of her charms and feminine wiles of every sort.

While she was still occupied with this person, so that she could no longer keep watch on the door, the bell had been pulled by a telegraph messenger, who was looking for an address because he could not deliver a telegram. Vigottschinsky was immediately down at the door, and soon afterward the messenger was already running off along the house-fronts in pursuance of his duty. But my aunt, whom Vigottschinsky had left asleep, was asleep no more; she had awaked, and he found her in a struggle with the burglar.

LXIII

I SHOULD sooner have expected anything else
than to be awakened by Marie Stark just on the
morning after this. The last time I had seen the
bookbinder family, and that has already been
mentioned, was when I was climbing into the
cab after my proposal of marriage in the Harlans'
house. At that time I was ashamed of knowing
them.

I was ashamed of them still, until my megalomania was drowned in secret distresses, cares,
anxieties, and the rising floods of mire and crime.
But then I did not think of honest Stark and his
daughter, because I did not wish to increase my
torments to no avail. After all, it could not but
make me feel like a shipwrecked mariner who
should suddenly remember that he had sometime
or other set foot on a sunlit, peaceful green island.

In the book of Ecclesiasticus, the fourth chapter, there is a verse, the twenty-seventh: "Avoid
not thy neighbor in his fall." Are there many
in our day that can still measure this saying of
wisdom in its full value? However that may be:

[194]

to recognize it is a great deal, to live according to it is the highest humanity.

So much and no less signifies that which Marie and her father have done for me.

She told me yesterday, "You started up out of sleep and stared at me. In that moment I knew everything."

You must think of this circumstance, if you would appreciate Marie's resolute heart of gold.

She knew everything, knew that I was a participant in the theft and murder to which the sister of my mother had fallen a victim, and the news of which was just being disseminated in newspaper extras. She could not tell how far I was involved. And yet she said, while the shouting criers ran by in the street below, as she reddened and shyly caressed me a little, "Lorenz, you have had bitter experiences, and you have others before you. But save yourself for me. I will wait for you."

Will anyone attempt to ascertain what these words meant to me, spoken to me on that morning by Marie?

She went back and forth between mother and

me and did not leave us for a moment. It is thanks to her that my mother first learned of the affair a week later, and only from her in a softened form. She always told her that nobody doubted my complete innocence. Marie herself, strange to say, likewise believed that in her own fashion. Her slogan might have been: "innocently guilty."

At about ten o'clock Stark came up. "Courage," said he, when we were by ourselves. To me it was a miracle to see these two people thus suddenly standing by my side without a word of reproach, although fully acquainted with the facts, while I thought myself forsaken by God and man.

I wept alternately with the father and Marie, because either she or he had to keep my mother occupied.

Flight was not even thought of.

Silently it was assumed by us three that the bitter cup of penitence and earthly punishment must be drained to the dregs.

I should not have waited for my arrest, but should have given myself up to the law, had I not been deterred by a certain feeling of obliga-

tion to my accomplices.   I did not want to appear
to them as if I were perhaps trying to secure
better conditions for myself by being a hypocrite.
Then too, by giving myself up voluntarily I
should have brought on myself the suspicion of
playing the informer.

I wanted to spare others as well as I could,
but to be unsparing only of myself.

I was glad that I had a fever, that I coughed
and was shaken with the shivers.   Despite such
phenomena I had the feeling that the crisis of my
grave sickness was now past, and that I was on
the road to recovery.

I could not escape a prison sentence.   Yet I
had spent the entire night in my mother's apartment, which could be proven absolutely, and the
guilt of direct participation in the murder did
not enter into my case.

On this morning and in the company of the
Starks I felt as if I had taken a very long, dangerous journey and had only just got back to my
four walls.

I awaited my imprisonment with impatience.
I saw in everything that was to come the great
bath of purification, so to speak, in which I could

cleanse myself of the dust, of the poisonous substances I had breathed in on my journey, and which would heal my wounds and restore my vanished powers.

LXIV

Such was the result, but I had thought the coming cure not nearly so hard, the healing process much less wearisome.

Strange to say, I was all at once restored to my former sober discernment. My supposition was that it would hardly be a matter of hours until my arrest. For I was thinking of my aunt's friend the police commissioner, who had informed my aunt of my doings. In order to conceal from my mother if possible the procedure of the arrest, Stark was posted as sentry at the little window in the front room that looked out on the street, so as to notify me at once of any suspicious occurrences.

And after some time he actually came back into the room with the announcement that a closed cab had stopped, four or five doors up, and that three gentlemen in plain clothes had got out of it. So the expected and yet so terrible moment was approaching.

I had already been walking restlessly up and down for a long time, with my hat in my hand and my overcoat over my arm. Now I suddenly found myself embracing alternately Marie and the old bookbinder, and I could not have taken leave differently from my real wife and my real father. Here was my wife and this was my father. No doubt of it, this hour of direst need had welded us together for ever.

The gentlemen stepped up to me down-stairs in the narrow entrance, to which point I had gone to meet them. One of them was the friend of my aunt, who was commissioned to identify me. It was hardly necessary. I gave myself up with the words: "Here I am, gentlemen," and went to the cab hastily and inconspicuously.

I longed for my solitary cell.

"Are you sick?" asked one of the gentlemen.

I said, "I don't know," and strange to say, "I think not."

"I hope you will not be misguided enough to make a useless attempt to escape," said the gentleman who sat beside me.

Whereupon I replied, "You forget that I limp."

"Yes, his one leg is too short," said the friend of my aunt in confirmation.

We drove past the house of Melitta and her mother. The windows were open, and the baroness was watering the little orangery at the window with a green watering-pot.

Goodbye, goodbye, I thought, and my throat contracted, and my body was all one grievous bitterness. The cab rumbled into the Ring, and as I looked up I saw the whipping-post. Something like a rosy, ghostly vapor was circling about it. Was it the shade of a departed spirit? Thereupon, as in a vision, the stone pillory revealed itself to me in its true frightfulness. I felt myself chained to the rings and whipped till I bled in the presence of the whole city, while in the Harlan house opposite the householder, the family, and all the servants stood at the windows. And it seemed to me, apart from my own suffering, that all this was not so bad, but that the worst was a horrible and cruel face which was leering at me, and which a voice at my ear named to me, while I felt my heart turning to stone, as the true countenance of mankind.

When I looked up again, for mostly I kept my eyes fastened on our eight knees so close together,

I recognized a former fellow-clerk and desk-mate from the municipal office, who was going to the city hall to work. He had been my neighbor there for many years; he was a cheerful, contented soul, and he showed that now as he saluted a colleague with the gesticulations of John, the Merry Soap-Boiler,[1] before disappearing with him in the porch of the city hall.

Why am I not going up to the city hall any more, I wonder, contented and happy with these people? I thought. And wasn't it glorious when it so happened that we could go down into the huge basement vaults of the city hall for our lunch hour, and eat our Wieners and drink our beer there?

Why, there was a familiar driveway and built around it was, sure enough! the old house of Emmo Harlan that everybody knew. After all, I clung for a long time, the thought came to me, to the idea that the hardware-merchant would surely have to give me some answer to my proposal. I saw in my mind's eye how I had run after the carriage of little Veronica and been led

[1] Translator's note. A reference to a well-known poem en-entitled "Johann, der Seifensieder," by Freidrich von Hagedorn.

out into the street by the domestics, and how for the second time, befuddled by a sort of triumphant frenzy, my breast puffed up with the idiotic presumption, I had stepped out of the driveway and into the Ring. How did I come to do all this? And what a variety of previous occurrences accounted for my coming to drive with these gentlemen in a cab.

Suddenly I drew out my handkerchief, and before the police officers could prevent it, while my whole breast seemed to fill with hot tears, I waved it out of the window toward the flashing window-panes of the Harlan house. Of course the officers, who immediately drew back my arm, thought that I had done this to give my accomplices the "office," that is a sign.

For a time I was absent-minded and thought myself on a journey. Around me was a wholly unfamiliar city.

When I came to, the enveloping world had approached me in an oppressive manner. I perceived familiar things, of which I thought I had been dreaming the night before. I was to be taken to the so-called Inquisitory, as I thought I must gather from the remarks of my escorts. But this could not possibly be the Inquisitory. I should have sooner expected anything else than that they would bring me to this house, that I should have to climb those stairs again, instead of going to the peace and protection of my prison cell. Of course it lay with me whether I would make it a cell for prayer, for atonement, for saintly living.

But this was really too much. I stopped short in the middle of the staircase and asked if they had not made a mistake. The answer was: "Not at all." A hundred times I had climbed this narrow, creaking wooden staircase, without noticing anything special about it, for it was the stairway to Aunt Schwab's apartment. But now invisible fists, countless and terrible, struck out at me from the walls, from the coming darkness in front of me, and I did think of running away, come what might.

My companions must have noticed that, for they grasped me more tightly, and I stumbled, fairly hurled forward, into the vestibule of my aunt's flat.

The apartment consisted of the small unlighted vestibule, a cramped kitchen with a pantry, the room in which my aunt slept, the parlor with the red plush sofa, and the little office, which contained the many pigeon-holed cabinets for the deposited objects, the ledger, the correspondence, and the like. The little steel safe was not here, but was set up in the parlor beside the sofa, so that it should not meet the eyes of the many kinds of people who went in and out of the office.

For some seconds, while we were compelled to wait in the vestibule, I had the feeling of standing before an experience that would shroud my soul in eternal night, and then again I was as far removed from all that was going on around me as if I were a mere spectator looking on at a prearranged spectacle.

The morning sun shone into the office, the door of which was open. Also the doors to the parlor and the kitchen stood open. They had probably left everything as nearly as possible unchanged from the state in which they had found it after the night of the murder.

The canary from the Harz, hanging in the office, was singing loudly and incessantly with all his might. His thoughtless and carefree jubilation formed the strangest contrast to that which had transpired and was still transpiring here.

At the office-door something violent must have taken place. A clothes-tree which stood near it, with my aunt's raincoat and umbrella and, as I recognized, with Vigottschinsky's hat and overcoat, was overturned.

On the table in the parlor the remnants of yesterday's supper had not yet been cleared away. There were bread, butter, cold meat, radishes, Swiss cheese, and egg-shells, as well as a half-empty and a wholly empty wine-bottle. On a platter lay the bones and head of a smoked flounder, a dish which was distasteful to my aunt, but which she mostly set before Vigottschinsky because he liked it.

I shuddered slightly as I saw these victuals. Hard to say for what reason. Perhaps I felt as if a ghost-supper had taken place here.

But how, why did just this simple and most actual bread, this yellow butter, etc., seem to me quite especially ghastly? Whereas the murmur of voices behind the closed door of the bedroom hardly affected me. To be sure: the spectral world about me increased. An instinct told me that the increase of spectral elements in the field of my perceptions was actually an advantage to me. I only needed to help the process on a little, in order to take from the horrible, brutal reality almost everything real and actual, which might otherwise have destroyed my mind.

Incessantly I felt a nausea which increased several times to a convulsive retching. Because many a wrathful thought came to me, and I even gritted my teeth, I seemed all the more to my escorts as a dangerous miscreant. But I was merely seized with unspeakable bitterness in the face of that incomprehensible power which had held up to me the prototype of beauty, so to speak, in order to lure me with it, by craftily shrouded paths, into a stinking cess-pool.

But grinding of teeth and the lifting of clenched fists is of no avail. Man has an overweening conception of himself. He is reared in a lie and is naturally surprised when it is proven to him, with a brutal kick of fate, how little truth there is in his supposed equality with the gods.

But perhaps it was just as well that a grim defiance had come upon me at the very moment that the door of the bedroom opened, where they were going to confront me with the murdered woman, as of course I had long since realized. Without this defiance I might not have been able to bear up.

The officers and I were about to move forward, when they motioned us back and closed the door again.

A fit of nervous laughter seized me, which was naturally chalked up against me as callousness, as brutality. But a recollection from the days of my childhood had suddenly rushed into my mind, when we three, my sister, my brother, and I, had likewise waited in the utmost expectancy for the opening of a door. Back of it the familiar Christmas table had been piled with gifts, and the candles were just being lighted on the tree.

And I sobbed with convulsive laughter, because I could not help thinking how similar after all were the proceedings of this day, though to be sure a very different ceremony was to follow.

Meanwhile the door was actually opened wide. I collected my thoughts for a moment, and as we advanced I thought, as if mechanically, of nothing else but the words of my Marie: "Lorenz,

[208]

you have had bitter experiences, and you have others before you. But save yourself for me. I will wait for you."

No, I face about here. I will let the unreal shadow of my personality, my shadowy double enter without me across the threshold of the disgusting and in every respect defiled alcove where my aunt lay in her nightgown, a hideously degraded corpse.

Oh, roses, roses! One must inhale the odor of roses, of thousands and thousands of incense-bearing roses! Or the scent of the mountain stream that rushes along over yonder, cold and clear. The perfume of the pines! Steeling draught of the pure, heavenly mountain air, permeate me, be blessed to me as my daily bath!

Herewith let the resolve be taken to deliver up to my good Marie, to-day or tomorrow, even the picture of Veronica.

Strange how I suddenly hit upon that idea.

What connection between the shudder that has come over me this very day at the mere recollection of the murder-chamber, at merely standing before its imaginary threshold, and this little square of cardboard, from which Veronica's lovely little child-face smiles up at me?

What connection between this prototype of beauty, this heavenly and wonder-working image, and the stinking hell-hole whose very thought poisons the air of my clean house?

Well, no other than that between the beginning and end of a road.

I have reflected on the connection between this starting-point and this terminus in my cell, where I was under lock and key and had plenty of time for it, and what I have discovered in this way is to be sure only a small part, as I have shown.

Namely this: the sight of the utmost purity led me into the deepest wickedness, and the sight of the basest wickedness led me to purity, and even in another and better sense.

Did those magistrates dream, as they either furtively watched me in the presence of the dead woman, or stared at me, or tried to catch me napping with their questions, or snapped at me, that it was just in that den of murder and pestilence, just under that cross-examination, that there came to me with the power of a lightning flash the illumination that has lifted for me out of the darkness the world in which I am now living, and in which I shall live out my life till the day of my death?

LXV

I THOUGHT of striking out the foregoing chapter. But I will let it stand, because it bears witness to a certain confusion into which I can be brought even, to this day, by the recollection of my confrontation with the dead body and with Vigottschinsky at the side of it.

But I shall attempt to clear up the main point of the chapter, and thereby perhaps the others too, to a certain extent.

All at once, you see, the murder-chamber revealed to me the entire hopeless wretchedness to which all life is condemned. This revelation occurred, as I say, with the power of a lightning-flash, in a blinding, almost deadly light, as it seemed to me at the moment. There lay the dead woman, in whom the rigor mortis had already set in, almost naked and, it may be said, exposed to the eyes of all in a disgraceful position. This throttled female, with her ugly shape and her throat all black and blue, had not one feature that reminded me of Aunt Schwab. This mass of moulded flesh was so alien to me that at the sight of it I felt nothing but an animal shudder.

It was for this, then, that my aunt had piled up penny on penny, mark on mark, had figured and done usury, systematically exploited the misery of others, to come to this end, which of course she could not have ultimately escaped, even if the unchastity of her old carcass had not laid her in the arms of her murderer.

And was she really so very much less laden with guilt than he? Mother told of two cases where clients of my aunt had each in his own way committed suicide, when their notes were presented for payment.

Well, and these judges, these police officers, these prosecutors, could one pronounce them guiltless and sinless men? Have not almost all human beings a secret sin to conceal, a secret misdemeanor, if not many and positively criminal offences? And think of all that is done even by the courts, partly out of general human shortcomings, partly out of negligence or carelessness, whereby the happiness or unhappiness, the life or death, of innocent persons is decided!

So I went out of this room in deep penitence, to be sure, but on the other hand with a strangely exalted soul. It was as if I were lifted out of myself.   It was clear to me that provided I made good use of the insight I had gained, I could lose little, but could take to myself the true profits of life: the power of rising above one's existence, a power which is the equivalent of the power to renounce.

And now perhaps you will understand my resolve to part with the little photograph of Veronica Harlan.

LXVI

Now I have crossed the threshold of the murder-chamber after all, but only in imagination, and only passing over it back and forth in such a way that it could not but be clear how I went in and came out as two entirely different persons. After I had stood under the lightning-flash of my illumination, I saw the crude deceptions to which I had fallen a prey, about like one who thinks he is stepping on a green flowery mead and who sets his foot on a deep pit of liquid manure, completely overgrown with green duck-weed, in which he promptly sinks down over his head.

When I sat in my prison cell, behind bolts and walls and close-set iron bars, robbed by men of my freedom, I had gained an inward freedom, I had cast off the bonds and fetters of grave error. I had risen up again out of the manure-pit and had shaken the filth from me. I think myself safe from a fresh immersion of that kind.

There followed the trial, there followed hearing after hearing. The investigations brought to light things that were so remote from the true course of my experience that they are without significance for it. And since I had learned once for all how to separate appearance from reality, I kept on applying my learning, and the central core of my being was no longer touched by the external procedure of the trial.

At times during the sessions of the jury I felt as if my place in the dock were occupied only by a lay figure, on which judges and prosecutor were venting their rage, while I myself had stayed in my cell.

LXVII

A CERTAIN ebb in my communicative craving and in my material is setting in. So probably most of that which concerns the crisis in my life has gradually been told. And yet I feel as if something important had been left unsaid.

I shall go over to the school-house today to see Dr. Levine—he has repeatedly asked about my literary undertaking—and shall agree with him upon a day when I can read to him what I have written so far.

The peculiar thing about my case is that I am in accord with it, I mean my case. For this reason my memoir has overstepped the bounds of what might have been a defence before worldly judges. On the contrary, the judges that I take into consideration as readers are such as have outgrown the judge's calling on their own part. Such a man is Dr. Levine, of whom I have already spoken before. He is the quondam state's attorney, who is the village schoolmaster here, and who has no greater desire than to spend the rest of his days under the elders, ashes, and birches of our simple hamlet, and to end the dream of life some day in the densely overgrown churchyard of the place. In this as in many other points he and I are of one mind.

When I said I was in accord with my case, I meant that I am not one of those who have done time in prison, and who cannot get over grieving about it. Their ambition seems to have been made ten times more active, like the nerve of a hollow tooth, by the ineffaceable stain that adheres to them in the eyes of the community, and to cause them a thousand times more pain. They cannot get over saying, "Oh, if I only hadn't . . . oh, if I only weren't . . . oh, if I could only undo what has been done. . . ." Their existence is a chain of self-reproaches and repentances. They are almost maddened by the attempt to turn back the hands of the clock of life to the time that preceded the deed. How differently I should act to-day, they think.

"Tell me," I asked Dr. Levine, "why did you give up your legal career?"

"Law and rights descend from generation to generation like an eternal malady," said Dr. Levine. And he added, "Judge not, that ye be not judged."

I have also jotted down a passage from the patristic writer Tertullian which he translated for me. It shows how the early Christians thought of holders of power and wielders of power, of judges and courts, and reads thus: "Recently a dispute arose whether a servant of God might take over the administration of any post of honor or any office of authority. If we admit that anyone can do this without taking an oath, can act as holder of a post of honor without pronouncing judgment on the life and death or the civic honor of a human being, can promulgate a penal law without condemning someone to be chained, imprisoned or tortured—then even a servant of God may accept such an office."

No, I am not an "Oh-if-I-weren't" or "Oh-if-I hadn't." I am a believer in being, in living. Life is much too vast to be stowed away without residue in the humdrum retail store and back room, and I already know much too much about it not to feel firm and free and justified in it. Here is the sun, here is the moon, here are the stars, here is the Milky Way. I breathe air, fragrance, warmth, ice, fog, tempest. I enjoy the light, I enjoy the night-time. If they should exclude me from intercourse with the petty human fossils, well, what greater favor could be done me? But if they should promptly leave me entirely alone—well, after all, what human being is not entirely alone? And is my consciousness not unbounded? And should I esteem myself lower than humanity, lower than any living human being, when I am fervently pressing close to the Godhead every day and every night?

I have looked deeply into my case from every side, as I say, in the long nights and days of my solitary confinement, and finally and ultimately found myself in accord with it. The trivial, narrow-breasted, narrow-minded municipal clerk that I was is no more. My breast is arched, my spirit is independent and broad, even my walk has improved.

I will not gloss over ugliness, and yet one might use a rather bold figure and speak of a pearl that I had found at the bottom of the manure-pit and brought up with me. And without this experience-chain of disappointment and suffering, could I have known an hour like the one when I was released and stepped out of the door of the Breslau Inquisitory under the open sky, whereupon Marie was immediately clasped in my arms?—

No, I will not go over to see Dr. Levine. I shall not reveal the contents of these pages even to him. In the first place, there would be a certain shamelessness in it, the display of which I could perhaps not forgive myself for a long time. It would probably make me carry a discontent around with me for years to come. Who can tell whether that discontent might not assume proportions that would drive me away from here into a new and alien spot, simply because my secret, my most sacred and deepest secret, was in the hands of another? And of course I should have been exposing to public gaze the tenderest emotions of my father-in-law and my wife without their consent. "Why don't you write," my good wife did say to be sure, "perhaps it may turn out to be a book, you know." Well, it is a book by now, but my good Marie and Papa Stark might be startled after all, if they should see how far I have gone in the revelation of myself and of us all.

And yet might I not show it to them, either? Well, perhaps the time for that may still come, some winter day, some winter evening. For the time being I will lock the pages up.

It still remains to be considered, however, whether I should cause Marie's heart fresh pain by the revelations about Veronica.

I can easily put off Dr. Levine by saying that I had suddenly come to realize that the thing could not be done in this form, and that I must begin the entire work all over again.

My mother died before I saw the light of freedom again. I hope not of a broken heart, as they say. Besides Stark and Marie, my brother Hugo took care of her while I was in prison, he having been appointed as drawing-teacher in a city high-school by a strange agency, of which I shall speak. My mother never believed in my guilt, Marie and Stark say, and never lost her faith in my good character or in me.

Melitta only came to see me in prison a single time, but smuggled Veronica's picture in to me in a New Testament. I was deeply touched by this trait in her character.

Today I do not know nor care to know where she is.

My brother Hugo received his position, as I say, through a strange agency.

What I could not achieve with the very most ardent desire of passion, nor by distracting myself to the point of madness, namely to so much as speak with Veronica Harlan, that privilege fell into my brother's lap in the most natural way in the world.

Fortunately he had spent the period of my great crisis outside of Breslau, in Munich, in fact. He only returned to Breslau after the grass had long been growing over my trial. He had the best of recommendations from Munich, and so he received from the director of the Breslau school of art a so-called master-studio.

Mr. Harlan had applied to this director and requested him to recommend a talented young artist, who also would be suitable in respect to his morals, to undertake the instruction of his daughter Veronica in drawing and painting.

The choice had fallen on my brother.

It fell on him and was approved by Harlan, although the director did not conceal the relation in which he stood to me and my fate.

Harlan took a liking to my brother, and it is

[223]

due to his influence as member of the council that he was appointed, again in spite of me, as teacher in the employ of the city.

I have no idea in what manner my sister Melanie escaped the punitive hand of the law. I received a single letter from her, sent from Bahia in Brazil. She said she had married there. The close of the letter was: "If I get along well, I will write again two years from now. If not, goodbye for ever!"

HAUPTMANN'S DRAMAS

*The authorized translation into English thus far includes
seven volumes*

VOLUME I. SOCIAL DRAMAS

Before Dawn   The Beaver Coat
The Weavers   The Conflagration

VOLUME II. SOCIAL DRAMAS

Drayman Henschel   Rose Bernd
                 The Rats

VOLUME III. DOMESTIC DRAMAS

The Reconciliation   Colleague Crampton
Lonely Lives   Michael Kramer

VOLUME IV. SYMBOLIC AND LEGENDARY DRAMAS

Hannele   The Sunken Bell
Henry of Auë

VOLUME V. SYMBOLIC AND LEGENDARY DRAMAS

Schluck and Jau   And Pippa Dances
Charlemagne's Hostage

VOLUME VI. LATER DRAMAS IN PROSE

The Maidens of the Mount   Griselda
Gabriel Schilling's Flight

VOLUME VII. MISCELLANEOUS DRAMAS

Commemoration Masque   Fragments:
The Bow of Odysseus   I Helios
Elga   II Pastoral

Uniformly bound, each volume, $2.50

Published by B. W. HUEBSCH, INC., *New York City*